HELLFIRE TOWN

Duke Oakman was hell-bent on turning Chesterville, Arizona, into a haunt of crooks; in the Mexican quarter, Juan Garcia waged his own reign of terror. Most folks were too frightened to make a stand, but Merle Claymore, niece of the town's founder, was a fighter. Ethan Winter knew he had to stay and see it through with her to the end.

BRETT PASCO

HELLFIRE TOWN

Complete and Unabridged

LINFORD
Leicester

First published in Great Britain in 1992 by
Robert Hale Limited
London

First Linford Edition
published August 1994
by arrangement with
Robert Hale Limited
London

British Library CIP Data

Pasco, Brett
 Hellfire town.—Large print ed.—
Linford western library
I. Title II. Series
823.914 [F]

ISBN 0–7089–7586–0

Published by
F. A. Thorpe (Publishing) Ltd.
Anstey, Leicestershire

Set by Words & Graphics Ltd.
Anstey, Leicestershire
Printed and bound in Great Britain by
T. J. Press (Padstow) Ltd., Padstow, Cornwall

This book is printed on acid-free paper

1

THE town of Chesterville, Arizona, just twenty miles from the Mexican border, was a beehive of noise and movement on this bruisingly hot June afternoon. Main Street swayed under the jostling mass of bearded teamsters and spur-clanking cowboys, passing shop doorways where merchants stood belligerently watchful with folded arms.

Ragged urchins dodged through the crowd, and two Mexican beggars squatted on the steps of the bank building, hoping to catch the eye of those frock-coated dudes bound for one of the saloons. The gaudily dressed saloon girls lounging in door fronts were after the same customers as the beggars, only with more guarantee of success.

A choking dust cloud billowed up as a trio of whooping rangehands tore wildly through the street traffic, panicking a leisurely Mexican burro train. The offended braying of the burros increased the din, and a few shots were loosed off in the air, as the riders reined up outside a ramshackle Chinese eating house.

To the man emerging from the Wells Fargo depot at the end of the street, the scene was a confusing riot. Dark-dressed in city garb, he was sweat-soaked and weary from his bumpy journey from Tucson, a good few miles north of here.

The dust-filled air was hot and stifling, leaving a sour grittiness in his mouth and Ethan Winter felt stiffer than a man not yet thirty had any reason to. As the stage which had brought him here rattled off, he set down his heavy carpetbag, and wiped his forehead.

Someone tapped him on the shoulder. Jerking round, he saw the skinny depot agent. "Forgot your change, mister. It's only a quarter for minding your trunk."

Ethan Winter pocketed the coins. "Can't help feeling that the stage driver's dropped me in the wrong place. You're sure that this is Chesterville?"

The agent gave a high-pitched laugh. "Where else'd it be, mister? Nowhere else to go between here and Mexico, 'cept a few adobe villages."

"Not how I remember it," breathed Ethan. He kept his eye on what was going on down at the eating house. *Charley's Place*, it was called, with a few battered paper lanterns hanging crooked round the sign.

He didn't like the way an expectant crowd was gathering outside the eating house. Those three riders had gone inside, and he sensed the tang of trouble in the air. He remembered Charley Lo well enough. The little Chinaman had come here to help in his brother's laundry, then like so many of his race had saved enough to set up his own place.

"You been here before?" asked the clerk.

"Sure I have," said Ethan. "But I've been back in Chicago for a couple of years . . . " He paused, "Had some family business to see to."

"Chicago?" The clerk gave his braying laugh. "Place like Chesterville's bound to seem kinda different, then."

"How long have you been here?"

The agent shrugged, "No more than a couple of months. It's a rough kind of town. Mind you, the north side of Main Street's the roughest. Kinda strange the way the town splits like that."

Ethan gave a nod. He saw what the clerk meant. On this side of the street were all the stores; gunsmith's, feed-merchants and the like, the Wells Fargo depot and the bank. All the saloons, more than seemed possible, were over the other side, backing onto the sprawl of the Mexican quarter. Sure, there were a couple of cheap lodging houses, too, either side of Charley Lo's place, but it was mostly given over to gambling and drinking.

"I can't figure it," Ethan put his hat back on. "Not half so many saloons when I was last here. And those were kept under control. No shooting in the streets, either."

The agent laughed disbelievingly. "No shooting? I'd say that there's at least one serious gunfight a week. Only last week two fellers got holes blown in them. Right over there outside Schneider's Bar."

The more he saw and heard, the more uneasy Ethan was becoming. He stared beyond the scuffling crowd to the large hotel dominating the other end of Main Street, straddling the intersection of two other roads.

Along the one leading from the riverside and the bridge he saw a heavy wagon loaded down with timber throwing up a rolling dust cloud as the mule team hauled it on its creaking, groaning way into town. The other road, south to the border, was empty of any traffic.

Sarita's village was that way; not

much more than a huddle of brown adobe buildings. He'd spent a lot of time on the endless journey down from Chicago thinking about the beautiful Mexican girl: her dark eyes set in a face which could be so solemn and mysterious sometimes, and so sparkling with life at others.

He'd always felt bad about leaving everyone like he had, but most of all about walking out on Sarita. At the time, though, he'd seen no choice. Not that he'd planned on staying away so long; just a couple of months, maybe.

It hadn't turned out like that, though, and over two years had passed. For now he dragged his mind away from wondering about Sarita. Instead he voiced another question going through his head as he contemplated the hotel. "What in hell's gotten into him to let this happen to his town?"

"Who you talking about, mister?"

Ethan turned on him, "Who do you think? Chester Dale. The man who started this town thirty years ago."

"Sure . . . " said the man, backing away some under the other man's fierce gaze. "Sure, I heard of him, but . . . "

Something was wrong, Ethan knew it, but he stopped himself from saying any more to this man. By his own account the clerk was little more than a stranger here. He'd know nothing of the efforts that Chester Dale had put into building up the town he'd named after himself.

Some towns grew naturally, over time. Chester had forced this one into existence. He'd built up a successful shipping business in New York; then one day, still less than forty years old, he'd just sold everything up, and brought himself down here to Arizona.

By all accounts there wasn't much here, then; just a few scattered Mexican villages, and a run-down trading post by the river. Chester had bought up a fair-sized parcel of land, taken over the trading post, and set to his task of making a town.

He dreamed of the day when Chesterville would rival Tucson as a trading town. And he'd always been determined that his would be a peaceful, law-abiding town, worthy of a place on any map.

Chester saw himself as the town's father and protector, and as it had grown he'd kept a firm hand on things. There'd been signs of approaching trouble just before Ethan left, though. The wilder frontier towns in Arizona and Texas were getting tamed, with their rougher troublemakers moving out and looking for somewhere else to roost.

But Ethan had always reckoned that Chester would see to it that they didn't bring his town down. It looked very much as if something had gone wrong there and that Chesterville was going downhill fast.

Purposefully he picked up his carpet bag, and stepped away from the depot. If he was looking for answers, he'd likely find them at the hotel at the far end of the street. He'd only taken a few steps, though, when there was a flurry of activity from Charley's place.

Those three riders had emerged, and they were dragging the small, wiry figure of Charley Lo with them. He was kicking and struggling, but he was no match for the burly cowboys. More folk flooded over until the street was a seething mass of people trying to get a better view.

Ethan made his way swiftly now; his aches forgotten, though the weight of his bag slowed him down some. One of the range-hands had pinned Charley down, while another of the men deftly knotted a rope round his ankles.

Reaching the edge of the crowd, Ethan began to push his way through. Then he stopped, as he saw the sun glinting off a star pinned to a cotton plaid shirt. The sheriff was just standing there, thumbs hooked in his belt.

"Your boots nailed to the ground, sheriff?"

The lawman was overweight, with his

gun-belt slung low on his Levis below his sagging paunch. He studied Ethan with pale, watery eyes. "What's that you say, stranger?"

Charley let out a yelp of pain as the rope was pulled tight round his ankles. Ethan glared at the sheriff. "Seems to me that you ought to put a stop to that!"

"What's it to you? All the boys is doing is having themselves a little fun."

From someone nearby there was an acid laugh. "They're Triple-O boys, mister. Sheriff Cutler ain't going to bother them. More than his job's worth. Hey, sheriff?"

Cutler turned sharply, but couldn't see who'd spoken so he jerked his attention back to Ethan. "You just watch to your own business, stranger," he growled. "Else it might be you'll find yourself filling a cell tonight."

"You should take a close look at yourself in your shaving glass next time you bother to shave," Ethan snorted contemptuously. "If you've got any remorse left in you, then maybe you might be ashamed."

"Now you look here!" blustered Cutler, but Ethan was in no mood to listen to him. Turning away, he thrust through the crowd, using his heavy bag to clear a path for himself.

The words of that bystander had unsettled him. The Triple-O ranch was owned by Duke Oakman; it was the biggest spread in these parts.

And it was Oakman who owned the timber mill on the west side of the river. By some quirk of nature the slopes and ridges above the river had plenty of forest cover. Chester had always believed that the timber was too tricky to get at, and had never interested himself in that land.

But timber was like gold in this region, and, seeing the possibilities, Oakman had bought the land for next to nothing. It was a dangerous place to work, and several of his Mexican workers had been killed or maimed in the efforts to fell the trees and drag them down the treacherous slopes to the sawmill. That didn't worry Duke Oakman, though. Profit, even with blood on it, was still profit.

And he had a very different vision of the town's future from Chester. The frontier had a shifting, shiftless population of trail-hands, trappers, hunters, gamblers and gunmen with money burning holes in their pockets. A town with plenty of saloons, and other dubious attractions was what they wanted.

Chester had been determined to stop the unscrupulous upstart from buying too large a slice of Chesterville and corrupting it for his own ends. So it was more than worrying to hear it suggested that Oakman owned the local sheriff.

"You watch who you're shoving, feller!" The stranger glared at him resentfully but Ethan barged on regardless to the front edge of the crowd.

The Chinaman's ankles were tied good and tight now, and one of his tormentors was looping a rope over the jutting out bar from which the eating house sign hung.

"What in hell's name you think you're doing?"

Charley Lo recognised him at once. He wriggled hopefully, "Mister Winter, you come back."

Taken aback, the three men gaped at the newcomer. But the one with the rope, his bony face as brown as walnut, let out a whooping laugh of recognition. "Well, look what the wind's blown in, boys. Good ol' Ethan's back!"

Setting down his bag, Ethan took a couple of steps forward. "So you're still around, Hicks."

He'd rubbed up against Curly Hicks on more than one occasion. Called himself a cowboy, but the kind of work he did for Duke Oakman rarely had anything to do with range-riding. He was as mean as a wounded wolf.

Curly Hicks leered menacingly. "Not

13

forgotten me, then, Ethan Winter?"

"No way I could forget an ugly face like that, Hicks. Now you just let Charley go."

Charley writhed anxiously. "You take care, Mister Winter. I not want you get hurt."

"The Chink's got sense, Winter!" snarled Hicks, shooting a glance down at Charley. "He don't mind being strung up like one of his lanterns, do you Chinkie? It'll remind him to pay his dues like everyone else."

"I already pay you!" protested Charley.

"That's not what Mr Oakman says," said Hicks.

"What's all this about dues?" Ethan demanded. "As far as I recall it, Charley bought this place off Chester Dale. Is that right, Charley?"

"Right, Mr Winter. Pay all money I save to buy place from Mr Dale."

"Nobody asked you to speak, Chinkie!" snapped Hicks.

"Since he doesn't pay rent," persisted Ethan, "then what's this about dues?"

14

Hicks's companions were getting restless. "Who is this dude, Curly? Why you wasting time talking to him?"

"Seems Winter don't know how things are here now ... " Hicks spat onto the dusty ground. "Town taxes. Charley ain't paid, so he gets a little reminder. Few hours swinging in the sun by his ankles and he won't forget next time."

"Oakman's collecting taxes?" Ethan whirled to look at the crowd behind him; he tried to find a friendly face but could see none. What's going on in this town? There's only three of them. Why don't you try stopping them, instead of watching like a lot of hungry buzzards ... "

They all shuffled uneasily. Then he saw a face that he did know. "Joey Roberts, is that you?"

The kid had grown up a lot since he'd last seen him. Chester had given him a job at the hotel, doing general odd jobs, fetching and carrying. Chester had been set on training him to learn a proper trade in the hotel business.

Joey ran a hand through his tousled brown hair. "Howdy, Mr Winter," he mumbled. "How've you been?"

"What's going on, Joey?"

If Joey had been going to answer, he missed his chance, as the men behind Ethan jumped him. A spearing pain went through him as an arm went round his neck, and a knee was crunched brutally into his back. He pitched forward, his face ploughing into the stony dust, and the crowd scattered away. He barely had time to roll onto his back, when a boot-toe lashed viciously into his side, winding him.

Retching, he was dragged to his feet by his coat lapels. Hicks held him for a moment, and he felt sour, whisky-heavy breath on his face. Then Hicks thrust him away and he stumbled back against another of the men.

They played with him like that for a moment or two, shoving him from one to the other; he was too dizzy and winded to manage to put up a struggle.

Then as he fell back towards Hicks for about the fourth time, he sensed rather than saw a bunched fist swinging savagely towards his head. He buckled at the knees and the blow sailed harmlessly over him. Summoning all his strength, he hurled himself at Hicks, low down, grabbing him round the legs and pulling him over.

It was only a brief moment of triumph. Another of the attackers came at him from behind again, dragging him round by his hair, and lamming into his midriff with a punch which left him sagging like a busted bag.

Just as Ethan managed to straighten up, a couple of ferocious punches rocked him back, with his jaw throbbing, and blood pulsing from a badly split lip. Three shapes came at him as he stood there unsteadily, his vision blurred by a red whirling fog. If they carried on like this they'd likely kill him. He must've been mad to start this.

They were closing on him. Ethan braced himself as best he could for what was coming, and then someone fired a couple of shots into the air. The echoes had hardly died away when there was a thunderous, earth-shaking bellow.

"If you buzzards don't back off then you'll all be in wooden boxes by nightfall!"

Ethan sank limply to his knees. Not everything had changed in Chesterville then. Tobe Wellbeloved was still around. The unmistakable voice boomed out again. "You just get that Chinaman untied now."

Woozily, Ethan pushed himself back on his feet, turning towards his saviour. He had Ethan's carpet bag at his feet, and there was a heavy .44 in his right hand.

And that hand was as steady as the Rock of Ages. Unlike most of the present inhabitants of Chesterville, Tobias T. Wellbeloved had renounced the demon drink long ago.

He hadn't changed a jot since Ethan had last seen him. Tall and skinny, in shabby black, with a high beaver hat perched on his balding skull. He looked like a man who'd spend his Sundays preaching hell-fire sermons to an awed congregation, and most round here knew him as the Preacher.

And there was certainly a biblical blaze in his eyes right now. "You come over and stand by me, Ethan Winter. You toting a gun?"

"Haven't carried one since I left here. And didn't need to carry one here too often. Things've changed, Tobe."

"Daresay Hades was a quiet, peaceful place till Satan took over." He raised his voice, "You get that Chinaman untied good and quick, Curly Hicks!"

Hicks had been moving towards the wriggling Charley, but now he jerked to a stop. With one mind, he and his cronies stood in a line; each man ready to go for his gun.

"Only one of you, Preacher!" snarled Hicks.

Hurriedly the watching crowd began to move back. They wouldn't want to miss a juicy showdown like this, but no man wanted to get in the line of a stray slug.

"Just cool it down, boys!" The sag-bellied lawman pushed through the audience and stepped between Tobe and the rangehands. "You fellers'd better get back to the Triple-O. Mr Oakman don't want more killing than's needful."

"Outa the way, Cutler, else you'll get plugged, too!"

Hicks made to shove the sheriff to one side, but one of the other cowpokes stayed his hand. "He's right, Curly. Mr Oakman didn't say nothing about getting into a gunfight."

Curly snorted. "Don't reckon he'd lose no sleep if they was both to end up leaking like rusty buckets." But, reluctantly, he slid his weapon back.

"Come on now," ordered the sheriff nervously, "Jus' get yourselves cooled down, and back to the Triple-O."

Curly Hicks glared with a dangerous resentment, then followed his cronies over to the hitch-rail where they remounted, and rode off slower and quieter than when they'd come into town. The crowd began to break up too, knowing that the entertainment was finished.

"Real friendly of you, Cutler," mocked Tobe as the sheriff got Charley untied. The lawman shot him a sour look, and stalked off.

Charley Lo sat there rubbing his ankles. "Can't guarantee they won't try stringing you up again, Charley," warned Tobe. "You'd best pay whatever it is they say you owe, if you want to stay in Chesterville."

"He not want my dues," said Charley. "He want buy my place. Open another saloon, maybe."

"Another one?" Tobe shook his head. "One more nail in this town's coffin. If he wants to buy your place, Charley, you'll get no peace till he does."

"I stay a while longer." Charley eyed

Ethan hopefully. "Now Mr Winter back, maybe . . . "

"Don't you go getting your hopes up," growled Tobe. "This town's standing on the edge of a fiery canyon. One good push'll send it skittering into the chasm of Hell!"

Ethan, whose head was spinning, tried to think straight. "Tobe, what's happened to Chesterville? And where's Chester?" The world suddenly started to reel round him. Tobe grabbed him, stopping him from falling.

"You got quite a beating, son," he said gruffly. "Let's get you to the hotel. You'll find out about what's happened soon enough . . . "

2

ETHAN wasn't likely to forget the lobby of the *Royal Hotel*. He'd staggered in here, burning up with a fever, almost five years ago. Most men would have saved themselves the bother, and thrown him back in the street. Not Chester Dale. He was crabby, irascible, had a temper like a bear with toothache: but he never turned away anyone in trouble.

The hotel had never quite matched up to Chester's dream for it. Long before, he'd travelled to Europe on business, and seen some grand places in Paris. The *Royal* had been his attempt to bring some of that opulence to Chesterville.

This lobby was more like a parlour, though. There was a worn Indian rug on the floor, a large kerosene lantern suspended by chains from the ceiling.

French doors to the right led to the dining room, and there was a chewed-up wooden counter opposite, next to a flight of worn stairs.

The whole place had been shabby when he left: it looked twenty times worse now; dust coating every surface, a broken pane in one of the windows. The smell of decay hanging over the hotel yanked at Ethan's heart.

Tobe lowered the carpet-bag to the floor. "In the name of the Almighty, you carrying a ton of 'dobe bricks in here? This bag's all but wrenched my shoulder from its socket."

Aching all over, Ethan sank into a sagging-springed chair. "It's gold, Tobe."

The man sniffed. "Oh sure."

"I'm serious. Two thousand dollars in gold. Carried it all the way from Chicago."

Tobe blanched, staring at the bag. "You're crazier'n I thought, Ethan." He paused. "Come by honest, was it?"

24

Ethan leaned back. "My inheritance. Some of it, anyhow. There's a lot more back in the bank in Chicago."

"From your pa?" Tobe set to building himself a smoke. "You went back to Chicago to see him, as I recall."

Wincing as he pressed an exploratory hand to his side, Ethan nodded. "Got a wire that he was dying. Wanted to see me before he went to join the angels."

"You told us that much in the note you left," said Tobe dryly. "Told Chester you'd be writing, too."

Ethan shifted uncomfortably. "When I got there, things were kind of complicated. The old man was going crazy. My sister needed me. Someone had to take charge."

He hadn't been back home in over twelve years, since he'd run off. The lure of the frontier had proved too strong for a fourteen-year-old boy who had no hankering to spend his life running a boot factory. Every time he saw one of those fancy stitched boots being finished he wanted to be wearing them, not making and selling them.

The romantic dream had soon turned into harsh reality. For a while he'd lived like a coyote; bone-picking on the high plains in the wake of the buffalo runners. He'd worked in a Dodge City saloon, adding to the pittance the saloon-keeper paid him by robbing drunks.

In the end, though, he graduated from that tough wrinkle-bellied school, and it wasn't so long before he was pulling on a pair of those self-same boots that were being turned out in their thousands in his pa's factory, and riding that same range he'd read about in story books.

Tobe interrupted his thoughts. "Seems that your pa took a considerable time joining the angels, then?"

Ethan gave himself a little shake. "Always seemed just on the edge. While I'm going half crazy, running a business I reckoned I'd escaped for good'n all."

26

He shrugged. "No way I could come back till it was settled. Factory's been sold up now, though."

"And why in the name of the Almighty didn't you write and let folk know what you were doing?"

"Kept meaning to, but ... " He could make excuses until hell froze over, but there were too many other things to say. "He's dead, isn't he, Tobe? Chester's dead."

There was no other possible explanation. The rundown, deserted hotel, the town gone wild, Oakman's boys doing as they pleased. Tobe sat down on another of the chairs, laying his beaver hat on the floor. "Sure, he's dead."

Maybe it was almost a relief for Ethan to have it confirmed. If Chester had still been alive, and had let his town go the way it had gone, then he wouldn't have been the Chester Dale that Ethan remembered. "What took him off?"

"Heart attack," said Tobe promptly.

"Chester's heart was strong as a buffalo's!"

"And look what happened to the buffalo." Tobe gave a shake of his balding head. "Died in his sleep. Doc said he wouldn't have suffered none."

"How long ago?"

"Ten, eleven months, I guess. Would've let you know, Ethan. But you didn't leave no address."

"No, I didn't. Guess it was some funeral, Tobe."

"Big enough," the other man agreed. "Chester got seen off how he'd have wanted, I guess."

Ethan shook his head. "Guess it hit you pretty hard, Tobe. You'n Chester knew each other a long time."

"Right from when all this started," Tobe nodded.

Chester had always been good at saving folk from themselves. He'd found Tobe in that long gone trading post, set on using his last few dollars to drown himself in cheap rye whisky. His hope of staking himself a claim to a rich silver mine in Arizona had come to nothing.

But he'd been a builder and a carpenter up north, and Chester knew he'd found a man who could help turn his dream of making a town into a solid reality. This hotel had been the first building, rising where the trading post had stood.

Suddenly, Ethan's thoughts jerked away from the past. "The town's gone to the devil in less than a year?"

Tobe watched smoke meander to the cracked ceiling. "Headed that way before you went," he reminded Ethan. "What with Tucson getting a new marshal, kicking out the riff-raff. Some went to Tombstone. A lot more came here."

He eyed Ethan reflectively. "Though maybe Chester was to blame for the way things've gone since he passed on."

"Hell, Tobe, how'd you make that out?"

"Took too much on himself," returned

Tobe sharply. "Like for years this town never had no sheriff. Chester saw someone doing wrong, he poked a sawed-down shotgun in their face and fined 'em on the spot."

"Might be worse ways of doing it," Ethan observed.

"Sure, but it wasn't so easy as the town growed," commented the other man. "See, Chester looked after folk and they did what they were told." He shrugged, "So when he died those same folk were like headless chickens. Running in circles going nowhere."

"And that's when Oakman started taking over?"

"Who else?" said Tobe. "Chester's hardly cold in his grave afore Duke Oakman's calling a town meeting. Says it's 'bout time Chesterville got itself some democracy . . . "

He gave a grim smile, "With his roughnecks crowded round the walls, wasn't nobody about to argue. So we had us some elections. For mayor, sheriff, and a town council."

"Real democratic, then?"

"Well," drawled Tobe, "Duke Oakman's the mayor. You seen the upstanding feller we got as sheriff. And the town council's got some real fine members. Curly Hicks for one."

Ethan stared, "Hicks is a councilman?"

"Sure is," Tobe confirmed. "Though I wouldn't worry too much about it. Council's only met once to decide on the town taxes. Course, they all go into Oakman's pocket."

Remembering what Charley had told them, Ethan said, "And if they can't pay, he buys up the property from them?"

"You got it," replied Tobe. "Chester built the town, and sold it off to those who moved here. Now Oakman's doing his darndest to buy it all off 'em. I mean, you seen it. Owns most of Main Street on the north-side."

"This isn't right, Tobe. It can't be. What does the territorial government think about this?"

Tobe rubbed his chin, "Prescott's

31

a long way from here. And I guess they ain't too fussed that Chesterville's going to the bad. Maybe it does have more'n its share of villains, but keeps 'em out of everyone else's hair, don't it?"

He paused, "Now, let's take a look at those bruises of yours. Damn fool notion, taking on Curly Hicks unarmed."

Ethan waved him back. "I got another question for you, Tobe. I reckon you'll know what it is."

"I figure I can guess . . . "

"You seen her lately, Sarita?"

"Not recent."

"She's moved on? Maybe got herself wed?" He reached up, taking hold of Tobe's sleeve. "You can tell me, Tobe. A girl like that, she wouldn't wait for ever."

Tobe rested a hand on his shoulder. "She waited for you, Ethan. Always knew you'd come back to her." He let out a shuddering sigh. "Just wish you'd come back a mite sooner. Maybe . . . "

he shrugged, "then just maybe . . . "

Ethan tugged more fiercely at the coat-sleeve. "Tobe, you've got to tell me!"

"Six, seven weeks ago, it was," said Tobe slowly. "We got some renegade Apache roaming round these parts . . . "

"Geronimo, you mean?"

Tobe shook his head. "Not Geronimo. Young buck called Cuchua and maybe a dozen hotheads who cut out from the San Carlos agency a while back."

"They attacked the village? Is that what you're saying, Tobe?" There was a roaring noise in Ethan's ears; he kept his eyes fixed on that bony face.

"Just after sundown one night. I guess they was only after the livestock, what there was of it, but the Mexes put up a fight. Trouble was, Ethan, wasn't too many young ones there. Old men and women mostly . . . "

"And Sarita?"

"Sure. Sarita was there." He paused, "They didn't stand a chance 'gainst

Cuchua. He's a mean, cunning varmint."

There was a kind of mist in front of Ethan's eyes; and through it he saw Sarita's lovely face smiling at him. Ethan could sense the warmth of her, smell the musky scent of her as she reached out to him.

Then he heard someone let out a wild roar of anguish; and though he didn't recognise that unholy howl, he knew it must be his own voice.

★ ★ ★

He could hear Tobe clattering round in the hotel kitchen, singing tunelessly while he got some supper cooked up. Ethan couldn't put a name to the song, but then he wasn't listening too hard.

He was remembering how he'd first met Sarita Gomez. He was still weak as a new-dropped calf from the fever. His first day out of bed, and he'd been sitting in one of these very same armchairs, chewing the fat with Chester.

Ethan hadn't planned on staying in Chesterville longer than it took him to recover from the fever-weakness. He was set on heading for Texas; already he could feel that itch to be back in the saddle, feeling the sweat soaking his shirt, the dust burning his eyes. But Chester had a way of getting a man to spill out things he'd never meant to say like they were beans scattering from a burst sack.

Their conversation had been reined in by Sarita's arrival. She'd been working in the hotel kitchen in those days. Carrying a tray with some coffee and a plate of biscuits she'd just made, she'd looked like a vision of impossible beauty to the weary Ethan.

If he closed his eyes tight, he could see her now, tall and graceful in a red dress, with her thick, shining black hair brushing her shoulders. And her dark eyes looking straight into his, and them both knowing that there was going to be something between the two of them.

"Sit awhile with us, Sarita," growled Chester, "Ethan here's been telling me something real interesting."

"Didn't think I'd been saying anything of partic'lar interest, Chester."

"Maybe Sarita'll think different," Chester had retorted. He'd turned to her. "Remember your idea about starting some kind of school in your village, Sarita?"

"*Si*." She'd gazed at Ethan. "If my people could read and write like the *Americanos*, then life could be better for them. It is a poor village though *Señor* Dale has helped make things better."

Chester had been rewarded with that glowing smile Ethan had come to know so well, "My family and my neighbours they make some money from breeding horses. But it is not enough."

"I've tried to stop it happening, Ethan. But there's a rough, desperate *barrio* growing up on the north edge of Chesterville. Poor folk reckon they've got a better chance moving into town.

So they end up in the Mexican quarter, poorer and more miserable than they were before . . . "

"Education's not the answer to everything," Ethan had commented, unable to drag his eyes off Sarita.

"It helps," Chester had grunted. "Thing is, we just ain't been able to find the right man to help Sarita get a school started."

He'd suddenly slapped his hand on Ethan's shoulder. "Well, Sarita, this feller don't look much, but he's the one we've been waiting for! Any man who can spend his spare time teaching leather-arsed trail-hands to read and write can surely do the same for a few Mexicans."

Other men whiled away the boredom of bunkhouses, or nights under the stars with gambling, or drinking, or fighting. Ethan, despite the mockery he often got, would pull out a book from his saddle-pack. He saw nothing wrong in it. Hell, it passed the time.

It didn't take him too long to

discover that a goodly number of his fellow hands couldn't do much more than print out their own name. One day, someone got curious. "Reckon you could show me how to do that, Ethan? Show me how to make out those letters? I'd real like to write to my ma sometime. Let her know how I'm doing . . . "

Ethan had been too surprised to refuse. Over the next few years he'd taught a couple of dozen fellers how to read and write. His methods wouldn't have suited a normal schoolroom: yelling, bawling, sometimes even getting into fist-fights with his tough pupils out of sheer frustration.

Tobe returned, breaking into his thoughts. "Brought you some coffee, Ethan. Maybe you should get sobered up some before you eat."

Ethan shrugged. "I don't reckon I got drunk, Tobe." His eyes went to the near-empty bottle on a table nearby. "It just served to dull the pain some. If I'd come back a few weeks sooner, then maybe she'd still be alive."

Tobe shook his head. "And maybe you'd have been with her that night, and Cuchua would have got you, too."

"How'd they know it was this Cuchua?"

Tobe sat back. "I saw him, Ethan. Maybe an hour or so before he hit the village."

Ethan stared, "You saw him, Tobe?"

"Sure, though I didn't know it was him then. Saw these riders in the distance, a dozen maybe, headed south."

"You still living out there by the old church, then?"

"Suits me fine," grunted Tobe. He'd moved there years ago. Two or three miles south, it was an old mission; a couple of derelict shacks and a crumbling church long abandoned by its priest. And it was only a couple of miles north of the village where Sarita lived.

"Anyhow," Tobe went on, "I got a closer look with that old spyglass

Chester gave me once. You know the one I mean."

"I know it," snapped Ethan impatiently. "So you saw that they were Apaches? Did it seem that they were headed for Sarita's village? Wasn't there no way you could've got there to warn them . . . ?"

He let the stream of questions come to a stop. "Hell, Tobe I didn't mean to sound like I'm blaming you."

Tobe shook his head. "Don't think I ain't blamed myself. Looked to me like those Injuns was riding hard for the border. But they must've spotted the village, and decided to cut back at nightfall. Even if I had gotten myself there in time, one extra gun wouldn't have made a whole lot of difference."

"And you'd have been dead along with the rest of them."

The other man gave a grim smile. "When I heard the shooting start, I figured they might head back and deal with me too. When Apaches got fire in their blood they get a powerful hatred against the Christian religion."

"Your place hasn't been used as a church for forty years or more, Tobe."

"How's an Apache going to know the difference?" grunted Tobe. "Anyhow, I got my old Spencer loaded up, laid out the spare cartridges ... " He paused, "The shooting soon stopped, and then I saw the fire in the sky as they burned the village. Just sat and waited for them to come for me. Waited all night but they didn't come ... "

Ethan felt a tight band tightening round his heart. "And when dawn came?"

"There wasn't a whole lot left to see," said Tobe. "But I found someone still alive."

"Not ... ?"

"No, not her, son. Old feller with one eye."

Ethan nodded. "Manuelo. Little feller; built like a bantam, used to play the guitar." He swallowed hard at the memory of all his good times in that village.

"Don't know how he'd lasted the night," said Tobe. "Must've lost most of the blood in his body. Half a dozen bullets in him I reckon, but he'd crawled out of sight, and those savages didn't find him to finish him."

"Did he tell you anything?" Ethan asked thickly.

"Cuchua," returned Tobe curtly. "Kept repeating it."

"You think he'd heard the Injuns saying the name?"

Tobe shrugged. "That's what I figured. Anyhow, he died soon after I found him. And I buried them all. Would've taken too long to go for help. wouldn't have been decent to leave 'em for the coyotes and buzzards."

Ethan didn't want to think any more about what Tobe had found in that chill dawnlight. "Who in hell is this Cuchua?" he blurted out. "I never heard of the bastard!"

"You heard of Victorio?"

"Victorio? Sure, I heard of him." A shiver went through him. That Apache had been one of the more notorious members of his race. He'd fought a bloody war with army and settlers two or three years back, and there was nothing he wouldn't do to cause torment and pain to his captives. He'd finally been cornered down in Mexico in 1880, and finished off.

"He was Cuchua's uncle," said Tobe grimly. "And by all accounts Cuchua did some fighting 'longside him. Though he must've missed out on that final showdown."

Ethan didn't want to say it, but he did. "Guess this Cuchua learned a lot of lessons from his uncle?"

Tobe laid a hand on his arm. "Ethan, son. She's at peace now. Wouldn't want you tormenting yourself."

A voice spoke from the doorway. "If we had a fort near Chesterville those devils wouldn't have gotten away with murder so easily!"

They whirled round, startled, and

Tobe hoisted himself to his feet. "Only reason you'd want an army garrison, Oakman, is so you'd get a fat contract for building the fort, and running the trading concession." He glowered. "And nobody invited you in here!"

"Just checking up on my property," drawled Duke Oakman. He'd always been a fancy dresser. Today he was wearing a white and tall-crowned stetson; expensive hand-tailored frock-coat and britches, and a cream, patterned waistcoat with a gold watch chain hooked across.

There were three men behind him: the same three Ethan had tangled with earlier. From the way Hicks's hand was hovering over his gun, it was clear he was harbouring a good deal of twitchy resentment about having his fun stopped.

"This ain't your property!" Tobe barked.

"Not yours either, Preacher," retorted Oakman. "And it's only a matter of time before it's mine." He stroked a finger down his long nose. "Once Mary Claymore agrees to my terms."

"If she's got any sense she won't." Tobe glanced at Ethan. "Woman he's talking about, that's Chester's sister. Left her this place and the rest of his property. Taken her one hell of a time to decide what to do with it."

"And Oakman's trying to buy it off her?"

"The way I hear it," said Tobe darkly, "he's offered her half what this place is worth."

Oakman looked round disdainfully. "Right now, it doesn't look to be worth much at all."

Ethan stared at the man. "You cheating crook! Planning on setting up some high-class cat-house?"

"Can't see how I'm cheating her," said Oakman mildly. "Place isn't much use to an ageing widow woman in New York."

He twitched a hand at his cuff, "But you just mind what you say to her when she arrives . . . "

Tobe cut in, "What's that about her coming here?"

"Arriving tomorrow or the day after."

"That can't be right. Way Chester used to tell it, that sister of his hated travelling."

The diamond ring on his left hand flashed as Oakman reached inside his coat. "Maybe your pal had got his sister all wrong. Got this wire yesterday."

Instinctively, Tobe stretched out a hand. Oakman scowled, "Why should I show you my private correspondence?" But he thrust it forward. "Take a look if you're so eager."

Tobe took the flimsy paper. "Hell, I can't make it out. Looks like a spider with inky feet done a polka on it."

Ethan grabbed it. "Arriving Thursday or Friday to discuss sale of property. M. Claymore," he read aloud.

For the first time since arriving here he felt good about something. "Well, maybe this widow woman might get

46

more than one offer for her brother's property."

Oakman's composure deserted him. "What you talking about, Winter? No man in this town could best my offer."

Ethan shook his head. "I reckon I could, Oakman. Maybe you've got a bit of competition headed your way!"

3

"**H**AIL Mary full of grace. A little charity, *en el nombre de Dios*, and you will be repaid ten times over . . . "

Dark eyes watched Ethan hopefully from under a mat of tangled hair as the one-legged beggar held out a leather dice cup. Ethan mounted the bank steps. He wasn't in a charitable mood. He'd slept badly, haunted by nightmares in which he could hear Sarita screaming for his help.

The bank teller was just getting the solid door open. He cast a surly look at the Mexican. "I swear to God that some of them cut off their own legs just to get sympathy."

Ethan reached the top step and looked back. There was something disturbingly familiar about that unwashed, knowing face. He felt he owed the man

48

something for staring at him. "Wait till I come out and maybe I'll give you something."

"Then surely you will enter Paradise, *señor*."

"Maybe," Ethan grunted, and lugging the heavy carpet bag he followed the teller inside the bank.

Moving behind the counter, the man became efficient. "I don't believe we've seen you in here before, sir."

A rumbling laugh came from a doorway to the left. "I remember Mr Winter well enough, Leeker." A small, round-faced man, blinking from behind thick eye-glasses, was heading across the creaking floor, chubby hand outstretched. "When did you get back, Mr Winter?"

"Yesterday . . . "

"And been in a fight already?" There was a swelling bruise under Ethan's left eye, and his lip was still swollen. The president of the Chesterville Consolidated Bank tutted. "This town, Mr Winter . . . "

"Old place has certainly changed."

The banker scowled, "And how has it changed! Now you come on into my office, and we'll talk in comfort."

There was a warm glow about him when he emptied the carpet bag onto his desk. "Around two thousand dollars there. We'll take good care of it."

"Don't doubt it, Mr Shelby. Though I've got some idea on how I might start to spend it."

He related his encounter with Oakman last evening, and his thought that he might make an offer for the *Royal* hotel.

Shelby listened, a touch nervously, resting his hands on the money. "If Mr Oakman's set on buying the hotel . . . "

"If I outbid him," said Ethan, "not a lot he can do about it, is there?"

Shelby scratched the edge of his nose. "Well, I'm not sure. I mean, do you really want the fuss and fret of running a hotel, Mr Winter?"

Truth to tell, Ethan wasn't over-enthusiastic about the idea. Maybe he didn't care for Mary Claymore being cheated, but there might be better things to do with his life than spend it fighting Oakman. He gave a non-committal shrug. "I'll carry on chewing it over a while longer."

Ten minutes later and his business was done. The gold was locked behind a solid steel door, and he had a couple of hundred dollars in bills in his jacket pocket.

Shelby came out of the office with him. "A pleasure doing business with you . . . " He broke off, frowning.

The teller was arguing with a thin-built Mexican in ragged jacket and britches. A wad of bills lay on the counter. "I'm telling you, you can't deposit this here."

The banker strode over. "What's the problem, Leeker?"

"I've told him that we can't do business with him."

The customer turned, brandishing the money in Shelby's face. "Two hundred dollars here, *señor*. Honest money. I run honest business. Why you not take?"

"Against bank policy," said Shelby. "You people have got your own place."

The man let out a hollow laugh, and his dark eyes flashed. "You speak of Juan Garcia's bank? That is no bank, *señor*. He take our money and maybe we never see it again."

He caught Ethan's eye, appealing to him. "This make sense to you *señor*, a bank which do not take good *dineros*?"

"Seems kind of strange . . . " Ethan began. "And who's this Garcia you're talking about?"

"Nothing you need concern yourself with, Mr Winter." Shelby turned back to the Mexican. "Now, I'm afraid there's nothing I can do for you."

"You take his money, but not mine!" The Mexican waved an accusing hand at Shelby. "You think you are big *hombre*, but you no better than the rats in the *barrio*!"

He stalked out. Shelby looked uneasy.

"Perhaps this seems peculiar to you, Mr Winter."

Ethan reckoned he'd rather ask Tobe about this than get some rambling, self-serving explanation from Shelby. "You know your own trade, Mr Shelby," he said tersely, and hurried on out of the bank.

The beggar was still there on the steps. "You have been successful in your business?"

"Oh sure," said Ethan. He brought out some coins from his britches' pocket. Bending to drop them into the cup, he got a closer look at the grimy face. He let out a sharp gasp. "Micky? Is that you Micky?"

He felt winded, like yesterday when that roughneck had lammed him in the belly. This was Miguel Gomez, Sarita's younger brother. It could be her eyes staring out of these filthy, unwashed features.

"What in hell happened to you, Micky?" He remembered how this young man could straddle the wildest critter imaginable, as easy as sitting on a chair. Now one of his legs was missing from below the knee.

Suddenly the wheedling tone of the beggar had gone. "I was working on the timber slopes, a chain snapped, a log rolls onto me." He spread his hands, "My leg is crushed. Not the first to lose a leg, *señor*, not the last."

"You took a job with Oakman?" Ethan stared. "Sarita swore she'd never let any of her kin work for that crook."

"Times became hard." There was a flash of resentment in those dark eyes. "Sarita, she did not want me to go there, but it was better than begging. And now she is dead."

Ethan winced at the fierce accusation in the other's expression. "I never meant to stay away so long, Micky."

"Sarita she wait and say one day you return. Maybe if she not wait so long, and come live here in town, then she still be alive."

"Listen, Micky," Ethan blurted out. "Come have some breakfast. I got a hell of a lot of questions for you."

"I have nothing to say to you, *señor*."
A couple of dude gamblers were passing the steps. Micky put on his wheedling voice again. "A little charity, *en el nombre de Dios*, and you will be repaid ten times over . . . "

One of them barked out an unfriendly curse, and they passed on. But Micky ignored Ethan, who stood there for a moment, and then slowly walked back towards the hotel.

Tobe was heating up some coffee. He listened without comment while Ethan spilled out his story. "You expect him to greet you with open arms, Ethan?" He poured out two mugs of strong, bitter coffee. "They felt kinda betrayed when you cut out. I figured Chester for a crazy man when he hired you as a school-teacher. But he was right about you."

"Sarita made that crazy school work out. She could've managed without me." Ethan knotted his fists hard. "She was a better teacher'n me. Sure,

I cut out, but I left the school in good hands. And I keep telling you, Tobe, I never meant to stay away so long."

"And the longer you stayed away, the tougher it got to write a letter?"

"I guess that's how it was. Kept putting it off until maybe I figured it was too late." Ethan slammed his mug down, slopping coffee. "Then it was, and I didn't know it!"

He eyed Tobe wildly. "Things were fine in the village when I left. So what happened, Tobe?"

"Only so much I could tell you last night." Tobe measured his words. "You know how Oakman hated that school. Didn't want Mexes getting too clever. Labour don't come so cheap when it starts arguing back 'bout rates of pay and how things could be made safer up on the timber slopes."

Ethan nodded. It hadn't only been the villagers who drifted in to do a little learning. Word had spread through the Mexican quarter, and some days he and Sarita had found twenty of them there in front of them anxious to learn to read and write like the *Americanos*.

Anything which endangered Oakman's profits made him twitch like a dog with fleas. Ethan had received more than one threatening visit, like the memorable afternoon he'd given Curly Hicks a thrashing. After that, Oakman laid off.

"Once you'd gone," Tobe said, "Oakman got a whole lot more bullying. Any man who went near the village school lost his job, or didn't get hired. Sarita was tough, but she couldn't whup fellers like Curly, could she? And I guess Chester found that trying to stop things changing is 'bout as easy as trapping a spitting mountain lion in a paper sack. And he had Garcia to worry about, on top of Oakman."

Ethan frowned. "Second time I heard that name today. Just who in hell is he?"

The other man let out a tuneless whistle through broken teeth. "Guess you'd say Juan Garcia's the Duke Oakman of the Mexican quarter. Muscled in there last year. Runs his empire from the *cantina*. A Mex wants to scrape a living in that warren he can't do it without Garcia's say so. Even the beggars got to pay him for the privilege of begging."

"And Shelby's bank won't take their money?"

"Garcia runs his own banking system. And Shelby keeps out of trouble," said Tobe. "Course, Chester started wondering if Garcia and Oakman was in cahoots."

"And are they?"

Tobe shrugged. "Maybe they are, maybe they ain't. I keep myself well out of it, Ethan. Chester should of done the same. I guess the troubles in the village just about finished him . . ."

He paused, then went on. "See, Oakman bought up the land they was using for their horses. They tried carrying on, but there wasn't enough grazing. Just a few horses left at the end, and the Apaches got those . . . "

Ethan felt like there was a rocky lump in his chest. Hard times, Micky had said. "So folk started to slide back to working for Oakman?"

"After Chester died, sure, that's how it was. Or started drifting into Mex-town where Garcia got his fine-manicured claws into them. Sarita stayed put. Looked to those who stayed behind, the old ones mostly."

"Waiting for me to come back?" Ethan breathed a heavy sigh. It had been the wire from his sister; confused and begging which had dragged him away. He'd had no real feeling for his pa. But he'd always loved Gwennie and now she was pleading with him to come back.

He'd been a man torn between two women, and his sister had won because he felt he owed her something from all those years ago. Going back to Chicago was something he had to do, but he knew that explaining all that to Sarita, saying goodbye, would make it even harder for him.

So he'd ridden off, saying nothing: he was coming back soon, he'd told himself, coming back for good. But he hadn't returned in time to save Sarita, and he'd never forgive himself for that.

He spent the rest of the day in a kind of daze; trying to work things through in his head. Tobe's watching presence started to unsettle him. He sensed the other man was only staying around to keep an eye on him.

Ever since he'd gone to live out in the old mission, Tobe had kept his visits into Chesterville as short as possible. He only came into town for supplies, or, like this time, to check up on the hotel, which he saw as being in his charge until its future was settled. Doubtless he would have come and gone in an hour or so but for Ethan's arrival.

"I'm not going to shoot myself!" Ethan burst out, eventually. "I don't need you nursemaiding me, Tobe."

"Well you sure need something. You sit in that chair much longer and your butt'll get glued to it."

"Then I'll get my butt out of it!" snapped Ethan, glowering. "Maybe I should go get myself drunk."

"That's one answer, I guess."

Ethan shook his head. "Not the one I want. Hell, I'm going to find Micky. I reckon I ought to try making some kind of peace with him."

"Doubt he'll still be on his pitch now," said Tobe uneasily. "He'll be hanging out in the *barrio* somewhere."

"Then I'll go look for him there."

There was a warning note in Tobe's voice. "You just watch your back. *Americanos* ain't too welcome in there."

"Scarcely surprising, is it?" flared Ethan. "If everyone treats them the way Shelby does. And the way I'm feeling now, the man who sinks a knife between my shoulders'd be doing me a favour!"

★ ★ ★

He could almost feel the grease hanging in the air in this low-ceilinged eating house. There were no other customers in the dimly-lit hovel. "Anyone here?"

She emerged out of the tallow-flickering shadows at the back, near to a blackened wood-burning stove. She was a huge woman, with more chins than any man would care to, or dare to, count. From the look of her features, Ethan judged that there was some Apache blood in her. She wasn't the first half-breed he'd seen this evening.

"Garcia collects dues in this part of town," she grunted. "You tell Mayor Oakman that!"

His search for Micky had proved tougher than he'd imagined it would be. Like Tobe had suggested, this decaying warren of alleys wasn't the safest place for an *Americano* to be wandering alone. His questions were greeted with suspicion, sometimes with fear. Most shied away.

Things had looked kind of dangerous in the *cantina* he'd entered a few minutes ago. It had been noisy, smoky and ill-lit. He'd been approached by one of the girls, hurdy girls they called them, who worked there, evidently set on striking a bargain for her favours, but she'd been pushed aside by a huge Mexican.

"Garcia not want your kind in here, *señor*. You go now before you get hurt."

"Maybe Mr Garcia'd like to come out'n tell me that himself!" But he'd decided to quit being so foolhardy when two more large men had appeared out of the smoke-curling shadows, and got himself out of there.

The eating-house woman was staring belligerently at him. "You still here, Mister. I said . . . "

"I'm not with Duke Oakman."

She spat on the floor. "Why should I believe you?"

"I'm looking for someone. Feller by the name of Micky Gomez. Works a begging pitch outside the bank. Got a chunk of his left leg missing."

She tugged at her raggedy shawl. "Maybe there's ten men'd fit that fine word picture, mister."

"And maybe there's just one. But maybe Garcia's told you not to talk to strange men."

Her eyes flashed. "Juan Garcia don't tell me what to do. Why you asking for this beggar?"

"I'm a friend, that's all."

She stepped closer and her eyes narrowed, "I see you yesterday, mister, getting kicked round outside Charley Lo's. Fool way to go on. But I guess that you ain't in Oakman's pocket. Sure, Micky comes in here now and then."

"Figure there's any point in me waiting?"

Her manner shifted a little to the cold side of friendliness now. "You want to wait, then you buy yourself something to eat, mister. I ain't a public bench."

"Sure. Something to eat. You got a menu?"

She shrugged. "Most folk have eggs and chilli."

It was a poor sales pitch, but Ethan figured it'd be wise to keep on her side. "Eggs and chilli'd be fine."

Sitting down at a rough bench table, he watched her lumber over to the stove. She slipped three eggs into a spitting pan and stirred them for a minute or two with a wooden spoon before grabbing a plate and dumping the eggs on it. Then she pulled a huge pan across and slopped lumpy reddish gravy over them, and added a misshapen cut of bread.

"You eat!" she said, and it was clear she was going to stand there until he started into it. It wasn't the worst meal Ethan had ever tasted; once he'd shared boiled puppy with some friendly Cheyenne, and he chewed into this in the same way, trying not to taste it.

"Chilli hot enough for you?"

"Sure," he managed to gasp, as the gritty gravy burned the lid of his mouth. "Sure, it's hot enough, ma'am . . ."

"You will not taste hotter in Hell."

"And maybe that's where this town is going." Ethan took a breather. "From everything I've seen."

The woman looked at him thoughtfully. "They say this was always an accursed town. In the old times the Indians shunned it as an evil place."

"I never heard that," he said, glad to have an excuse to hold off taking another spoonful. "How come you know about Indian legends?"

"My grandmother was full-blood Apache," she said, with sudden dignity. "Married a white man. I still got kin up in that fever-hole they call the San Carlos Agency."

Her face became hard as glazed ironstone. "No place to put a proud people. Being cheated by the agency traders selling them bad meat, or holding up supplies till they're starving, then charging double."

Bitterly, Ethan said, "So these relations of yours cut off the agency and take to slaughtering helpless folk . . . "

She loomed over him, a great lowering shadow. "Most of that talk is lies, mister."

"Like what Cuchua did out in that Mex village, that's lies is it?" he barked back furiously.

She let out a curious, rolling laugh. "No sense in arguing with an *Americano*. They only believe what other white folks tell them."

"You trying to say it didn't happen?"

She made no answer, resting a huge, threatening hand on his shoulder. "Now you eat!"

Reluctantly he took another spoonful. As he did so there was a voice from the doorway; a scrawny urchin poked his head in. "*Americano*, you look for Miguel Gomez?"

Thankfully Ethan dropped his spoon. "Sure. I'm looking to have a talk with him."

The boy grinned. "Come, I show you, *señor*."

"I'm right with you." He slapped a five-dollar bill on the table. "Real fine vittles, ma'am," and with his mouth still fiery from the chilli-peppers, he got himself outside, staring round in the growing murk for the boy.

He took a few steps along the cramped alley. "Where've you gone, kid?" Even as he spoke, he sensed danger. The boy should be waiting eagerly; ready to haggle over the price for taking him to Micky. Unless he'd already been paid.

An instant later the gun slamming into his ribs confirmed his suspicions. "Keep walking, schoolteacher," hissed Curly Hicks. "Else you won't be able to walk."

Ethan just stood there. He should have figured that Curly would try to get even.

The gun jabbed fiercely. "Just git moving, Winter."

"I'm moving!" But as he stepped

forward, he also twisted round. Curly grinned with satisfaction; there was the click of a hammer cocking. "Figured you'd try that."

Ethan poised to spring. Curly's finger was certainly tightening on the trigger: he had maybe two seconds before he'd be lying in the alley with a gaping hole in him.

Then a vast shape reared out of the darkness and a massive skillet came down on Curly's head. He pitched forward like a felled tree, his weapon skittering away.

The woman from the eating house stared down at his motionless form. "Maybe I should've let this gringo have you. But I got few enough customers."

"I'd sure hate for you to get in trouble with Duke Oakman over this," said Ethan, retrieving Curly's gun, and shucking the slugs from the chamber, before dropping it by the unconscious man's body.

"This is Garcia's territory, not Oakman's," she reminded him. "But you best get out of here now. Could be that this feller here, he got *amigos* waiting nearby. They'll come looking for him soon."

There was an odd scraping noise, and suddenly Micky himself came in sight, swinging himself agilely along on a rough wooden crutch. "You right, Lizzie," he said. "Two of Oakman's *caballeros* waiting at the far end of the alley."

He balanced against the wall of the eating house, and made to swipe at Curly lying there. "That one is a pig. I should smash his skull with my crutch." He shook his head. "But another time, maybe. Come, Ethan, follow me now . . . "

Minutes later and they were back on Main Street. It was night-time busy, with every saloon bursting at the seams. "You heard I was looking for you?" asked Ethan.

Micky leaned there, his face impassive. "I hear," he said. "Maybe it is better that you leave Chesterville. There is nothing for you here now."

"I got some good friends here, Micky!" snapped Ethan. "Friends who maybe need a helping hand. And I got money, too. Honestly come by."

"Charity? You offer charity and pity?" Micky glared.

"You've got awful high and mighty all of a sudden for a feller who sits begging from gamblers!" Micky's eyes flashed, but Ethan surged on. "Friendship, Micky, that's what I'm offering. You're coming back to the hotel with me. And if you argue, I'll yank your crutch away and carry you."

Micky glared, "You talk big, Ethan."

"I don't mean to." Ethan scratched his ear. "Listen, Micky. Sarita's gone. But I can try making things up to her my friend her brother."

At last, Micky nodded. "*Si*, she would know you are right. Always Sarita knew what was right."

Two minutes later, and Ethan was leading Micky in through the main door of the hotel. It was dimly lit in here with just a couple of smoky oil lamps on the counter. "Get a bottle from the bar, Tobe. We got ourselves a visitor."

He stopped. Tobe wasn't alone. There was a different smell rising over the dust and neglect: a sweet lavender kind of woman fragrance. She stood up, with a rustle of petticoats, quickly followed by Tobe, and another pale-faced man; young in a crumpled city suit. And she was something special.

Blonde-haired, tresses coiled high, her large, dove grey eyes gazed out of a smooth-complexioned, beautiful face. She was wearing a tailored blue suit with bell sleeves, and a froth of lace at the neck. Despite the airless heat, she looked cool as a well chain.

"You must be Mr Winter." She walked towards them.

The young man said urgently, "Merle, you should stay away from him. You never know what you might catch."

Ethan bristled on Micky's behalf. "She won't catch nothing from me, mister."

"I didn't mean you. I meant that ruffian with you."

"Cory, don't be so impolite." She was extending a hand. "I'm Merle Claymore. Chester Dale was my uncle. My mother Mary died two months ago. Everything he left to her now passes to me."

Tobe cut in. "It was Mis' Claymore sent that wire to Duke Oakman, Ethan. M. Claymore . . . "

"I figured that out already, Tobe."

The girl gave a little backward wave. "You already exchanged words with Mr Cory Boon. We're to be married." She shook hands with Micky. "Uncle Chester wrote my mother about you and your sister, Mr Gomez. Mr Wellbeloved has told me of your tragic loss. I'm very sorry."

Ethan cleared his throat. "How come you decided to come out all this way, if you're set on selling up?"

"If I had decided that," she said coolly, "then I would have stayed in New York. I've come here, because this is my hotel, and I intend to make it the best hotel in Arizona!"

4

"HOWDY there, Mr Boon. Sleep well?" Ethan swung into the hotel kitchen to see Merle Claymore's fiancé sitting there. He'd changed from his creased city suit into a check shirt and Levis, but they didn't look right on him.

The man greeted him crabbily, "I thought I'd been deserted. When I woke up there was no sign of anyone."

"That's 'cause there was no-one here," he slapped down his packages by the stove. "Everyone else was up round dawn. Anyhow, Miss Claymore she's driven Tobe back home."

"What? By herself?"

"Hell, no. She's taken Micky Gomez on as her driver."

Cory gave his neck a vigorous scratch. "And when did Merle decide that? She said nothing last night."

"Daresay 'cause she decided this morning."

Merle Claymore had joined them in the kitchen, as fresh as a dew-soaked prairie rose. "I'll need someone to drive me round, Micky, and to generally mind my horses."

Washed and shaved, and dressed in borrowed gear, the young Mexican looked like a human being again. There'd been no doubt about his answer. For this offer, Ethan reckoned Miss Claymore could count on a devoted servant for life.

Cory Boon was shaking his head. "I wonder if the sun hasn't got to her. Riding off without a word to me."

"Just doing Tobe a good turn, that's all. Saving him a couple of miles walk."

"I thought everyone round here owned a horse."

Ethan set to unwrapping the provisions he'd bought. "Not Tobe Wellbeloved. Maybe he walks everywhere 'cause he reckons he should use the legs the good Lord gave him."

"Religious is he?"

"In his own way, I guess. With him living right by a church, and folk calling him the Preacher, maybe it's kind of rubbed off on him."

Merle wanted to see the ruined church. She'd tried persuading Ethan to go with her, but he'd planned to ride out that way later on. He had to look at the remains of the village soon. He wouldn't lay the ghosts in his head by hiding from what had happened.

"If you want company," Tobe had said, "then just stop off at my place on the way, and I'll come with you."

"Something I got to do on my own," Ethan had told him. Now he glanced round. "Care for some fried bacon?"

The easterner gave an ungracious grunt. "Seems to me that everything anyone eats out here is soaked in grease." He scratched at his neck again.

"Bugs having themselves a supper party in your room last night were they? With you as the supper?" He got no answer to that, and after pulling off his jacket he set to slicing up some bacon into the hissing fat.

Then as he got some coffee going he said, "I'll tell you how to stop yourself getting chewed to ribbons. Before you get into bed, rub yourself all over with a good layer of grease. Bear-fat, that's reckoned to be the best."

"You can't be serious!" Cory Boon stared in distaste. "Coating myself in dripping will stop me being bitten?"

Ethan gave him a long, serious look. "Well, it won't stop 'em trying. But every time they land on you they'll just slide off!" Unable to keep his face straight any longer, he let out a hoot of laughter.

"Very amusing," said the other man with a sickly smile, which turned into a frown. "You're wearing a gun!"

Ethan shrugged. "After my run-in with Curly Hicks I reckoned it was time I got myself some protection. Called in on the gunsmith on my way back here." He slapped his hand against the pearl inlay on the butt of the .45. "Real fine weapon. You want to take a look?"

"I do not! Back in New York you can pick up a telephone instrument and talk to someone in Chicago. And here men wear guns while they cook breakfast!" His scowl deepened, "I only hope I can persuade Merle against staying. This is no place for a decent young woman."

"It will be," returned Ethan. He flipped the bacon slices over with a flat spoon. "If more decent folk move in, there's less chance of crooks like Oakman getting their own way. And your Miss Claymore seems set on staying."

"I've just thought . . . " The chair scraped noisily as Cory sprang to his feet. "Last night the old man was telling how he'd heard the Indians attack that Mexican village. That means his place can't be any distance from there."

"Not so far away," agreed Ethan. "Well, this bacon's nice and fried, Mr Boon. Maybe you'd fetch a couple of those plates from over there. Might need the dust blown off them."

Boon yanked at his sleeve. "Suppose those savages are still lurking round? If they see a white woman they'll go crazy. And nobody to protect her but a one-legged Mexican, and a crazy old man!"

"Tobe may be kind of eccentric, but he's not crazy." Ethan went to fetch the plates himself. "And if Apaches're set on wickedness then the colour of a woman's skin doesn't much signify to them."

The easterner looked contrite. "I'm sorry, Mr Winter, I'd forgotten about your friend."

He found a couple of plates and rubbed the dust off them with his sleeve. As he shared out the bacon, he said, "Cuchua's got no call to be hanging round there. Nothing left for him to steal, or kill. Daresay he's down over the border somewhere."

He slammed the plates down on the table, with a fresh loaf in between them. "Now set down and eat and quit fretting about Apaches."

Despite his mutterings about greasy food, Cory was soon making hefty inroads into his bacon. "I can't understand why there isn't an army garrison here. If they attack once they might do it again."

Ethan sliced himself a good-sized hunk of bread. "Well, Oakman's pressing for a fort. A lot of money in it for him. But the army's got its hands full further along the border. General Crook's a lot more anxious about Geronimo."

Cory's eyes narrowed. "The New York papers think Crook's being too lenient with the Apaches. I've read that he's ordered a lot of traders off the San Carlos agency."

Ethan didn't reply for a moment, remembering what the woman in the eating house had said. "I'd heard that the traders were cheating the Apaches."

"I wouldn't have imagined you'd have too much sympathy for Indians," said Cory.

"Didn't say I had," returned Ethan sharply. He wasn't about to give any credence to that woman's assertion that the accusations against Cuchua were lies. He'd massacred Sarita and her neighbours: the evidence was crystal clear. "But you won't get 'em staying on the agencies by starving and cheating them."

He chewed thoughtfully. "Anyhow, General Crook's got a lot of the Apaches on his side now, working as scouts, and all. He'll beat the renegades in the end, though in this rough country it's no easy job."

"I'm glad your appetite has returned, Cory." Merle Claymore had come in without either of them seeing her.

Boon almost choked as he swallowed his mouthful too fast. "I had to eat something!"

"Very good it smells too." She untied her bonnet ribbons. In spite of the heat, she still looked crisp and cool in her red shirt-waist and full cotton skirt.

Ethan got hastily to his feet. "I can

fry you some, ma'am, if you'd like."

"Please, call me Merle. And no thank you. But I will have some coffee." She smiled at her fiancé, "And finish your food, Cory."

She walked up to where Ethan stood at the stove. "The whole journey he was complaining about his diet. I declare, he's terrified of getting food-poisoning."

It was a gentle enough mockery, but Ethan detected an edge there that showed that maybe the girl had grown close to irritation with Cory Boon's complaining ways.

"You got Tobe back home all right?"

"Indeed we did. I took a quick look at the ruins. It's an interesting looking church. I intended to go on to see the village, but Micky . . . " She paused, "Well, I can understand his reluctance. You're still planning on going?"

"Later, sure," said Ethan in a hoarse voice. He'd suddenly received a flashing mind-picture of what Tobe would have seen as he'd approached the smouldering ruins in the early light of morning.

Merle broke the silence, maybe sensing his thoughts. "I intend to call on Mr Oakman this morning. To give him formal notice that I'm turning down his offer."

"Merle, for heaven's sake." Cory was glaring at her with his wide, pale eyes. "I really think we should talk about this now."

"I'm sure there's nothing you can say you haven't already said, Cory."

He waved a hand wildly. "This hotel, it's falling down, filthy. Nobody's stayed here since your uncle died. And who on earth out of that mob of thieves and cut-throats out there is going to want to stay here . . . ?"

She listened to him with a faint smile. "I'm sure they're not all thieves. Once the place is cleaned up, restored to life, we'll get plenty of custom."

There was a sudden jabber of noise from out in the lobby; excited women's voices mostly, speaking Spanish.

Ethan got there first, and stared out. Micky Gomez stood there beaming, as he leaned on his crutch, surrounded by a dozen Mexican women of varying sizes and ages.

"Ah, you found some ladies, Micky."

"Of course, *señorita*. When Miguel Gomez says he do a thing then it is done quick as that." He snapped his fingers, and one of the younger and prettier women, grouped round him gave him a smile of admiration.

"Merle, who are these women?"

"I asked Micky to find me some ladies who can help get this place cleaned up, Cory." She stepped past Ethan into the lobby, and in Spanish so flawless that it momentarily silenced the chattering women, she started to tell them exactly what she wanted them to do.

Ethan grinned faintly. Merle had a good helping of the same optimism which had kept her uncle going through the toughest times. She'd need all that enthusiasm, and more, in the days to come. He reckoned he'd like to stay around to see just how she got on.

★ ★ ★

"Well, I'm so sorry that my husband's not here to greet you, Miss Claymore."

Lucinda Oakman was a pale, wispy woman; maybe there was a hint of the Southern belle she had once been, before Duke Oakman had brought her down to Arizona. But it was only a faint echo, like the shadows of bright colours on a window drape faded by too much sunlight.

Ethan stood there awkwardly by the door. He'd sooner have stayed outside with Micky, who was minding the horses and the fancy rig Merle had rented from the livery.

He'd never been to Oakman's place before; though he'd seen it from a distance of course. Close to, the ranch-house of the Triple-O spread was a weird, unlikely place. It was a small stuccoed castle in smooth-hewed stone, wrought-iron, and expensive shipped-in marble pillars. Every one of the glassed windows had fancy Spanish-style shutters.

Ethan had known ranchers with thirty or forty thousand head of cattle who lived in small log cabins. Duke, however, had an inflated opinion of his own importance, and the house mirrored that completely.

This library they were standing in was undeniably impressive. The smell of polished cedar, and waxed leather, with books lining every wall, packed as tight as an infantry formation. It was strange to find this in the house of a man who'd been so determined to deny even the simplest education for his Mexican lumber workers.

Lucinda Oakman stood there vaguely, and Ethan recalled the stories about her, too. It was said that Oakman's wife was a whole lot fonder of good bourbon than a respectable lady had any cause to be.

"This is a beautiful house, Mrs Oakman."

The woman flapped a thin, distracted hand at Merle. "My husband modelled the interior on my grandfather's mansion in Virginia. It was ruined in the War between the States and had to be pulled down. Duke fetched that down here . . ."

She pointed towards the impressive fireplace, made of grey limestone, above which was a portrait of Oakman, youthful in Confederate cavalry uniform.

"He was a captain. Of course, I know that Arizona was with the Union, but it's all such a long time ago now."

Her eyes turned onto Ethan, still standing stiffly in the doorway. This seemed a kind of betrayal of Chester, entering Oakman's house, being civil to his wife. But Cory Boon was displaying a degree of sulkiness which wasn't healthy in a man. He'd shown no willingness to accompany Merle, and Ethan figured someone ought to.

"You're the man who taught those

Mexican peasants how to read and write."

It had sounded like an accusation, but he caught the flicker of a smile on Merle's features, and kept his response restrained. "Hardly call them peasants, ma'am."

She gave one of her fretful waves. "And you're friendly with that man they call the Preacher?"

"Guess you could say so," he said curtly. "Why you interested in Tobe, ma'am?"

"Did I say I was interested in him?" She gave him a haughty look, but then all of a sudden her manner became knowing, even sly. "I saw him in the cards, you know. A tall figure in a black beaver hat."

"That'd likely be Abe Lincoln," remarked Ethan dryly. One of the Mexican women who worked in the kitchen here had once told Sarita that Lucinda Oakman had a fancy she could read the future in the cards.

"Oh, I'm sure it wasn't him!"

declared Mrs Oakman. "He had a beard, you know, and this man was clean shaven."

"Tobe's often got a haze of stubble on his chin," countered Ethan, but Merle was looking interested in an amused kind of way and gave him a warning shake of her head.

"It sounds most interesting, Mrs Oakman. What exactly did you see?"

"A vision of hell," said the woman fervently. "So clear, and so frightening." Her eyes widened. "That man, the Preacher, was flying through flames."

"Tobe can do a whole lot of things," said Ethan, "but I never saw him fly." He grinned, "And he wouldn't thank you for seeing him in the cards. He's dead against gambling. Calls a pack of cards the devil's picture book."

"Well, that's as maybe," the woman retorted petulantly, "but I saw what I saw. A vision of hell. I told my husband all about it. He's a great believer in my readings. More than once I've seen things coming, which have happened . . . ”

“That’s enough, Lucinda!”

The angry bark from the doorway was followed by the man himself striding into the room. He hurled his hat down. “Talking nonsense to our visitors and you haven’t invited them to sit down or given them a drink or nothing.”

She looked at him tearfully, “But I don’t have the key to the cabinet, Duke. You took it off me.”

He gave a snort, “Just quit that silly talk. I’m sure you’ve got something to do elsewhere.”

Without another word, she scuttled away like a startled spider. Oakman turned on such charm as he possessed, throwing a quick scowl at Ethan, and giving Merle a bow. “I take it that you must be Mrs Claymore’s daughter, ma’am. I know that she’s a lady of . . . mature years.”

Ethan restrained a hoot at the cold way Merle received his advances. “My mother has passed on, Mr Oakman. By the terms of her will I’ve inherited all she owned, including the legacy left by my uncle."

Oakman straightened up. "I see. But you will know of my offer to your mother for the *Royal* hotel. I know how much that place meant to your poor uncle, and I assure you . . . "

"I'd be grateful if you'd swallow all that sanctimonious talk." Merle glared, "my uncle hated the ground you walked on, and I see no reason to indulge in drawing room chatter with you." She drew herself up. "I've seen the terms of your offer. Frankly, Mr Oakman, they smell worse than a skunk."

This time Ethan did let out a laugh. He saw Oakman's fists knot up by his side. Still, he kept calm. "I'm prepared to discuss this with you further, Miss Claymore."

Merle reached for her parasol. "This was just a courtesy call, Mr Oakman. To tell you I'm not selling anything. I shall re-open the *Royal* as soon as possible."

A hard note entered his voice, but he tried to smooth it out. "Well, you may be taking on a tougher job than you imagine, Miss Claymore. Chesterville is a rough town, and if you'll take my advice . . . "

"As I'm sure Uncle Chester would have said, this family don't need no advice from your kind, Mr Oakman!" With the sweetest of smiles she moved past him, slipping her arm through Ethan's. "We'll find our own way out."

★ ★ ★

Ethan could still grin about the stunned expression on the rancher's face a few hours later, as he rode down the border road. Though maybe it wasn't so much to be cheerful about. Oakman had bought up just about every piece of property on the north-side of town.

Chester's hotel was a symbol to the merchants and business folk on the other side. While it remained out of

93

Oakman's grasp then they could hope that the town mightn't be taken over completely. So Merle was offering a meaty challenge to Oakman, which he wasn't likely to ignore.

The horse was slowing down, and Ethan gave it a friendly tap with his spurs. It was a strong enough animal; good-tempered and reliable. But it was a livery mount, and he was fixing on getting his own beast.

He'd passed Tobe's place a while back, and he turned in the saddle looking back at the spindly bell tower of the derelict church. There'd been no sign of Tobe. Doubtless he was enjoying the peace and quiet: maybe taking a *siesta*.

Merle had talked about Tobe on the drive back. "I asked him why he chose to live in such a lonely place."

"And what did he say?" Ethan asked. "'Cause when I've asked him I've never gotten a straight answer."

The girl shrugged. "As far as I could gather, he hated to be reminded of all those years of hard work."

Well, Ethan reflected, Tobe had made precious few changes to the old mission buildings. Maybe he'd patched the roof up, fixed the door back on its hinges. But it was more or less as it had been when he'd moved out of Chesterville and taken up his residence there.

He was closing in on the village now; the houses were shielded from his view by some scrubby cottonwoods; with a similar stand of trees and brushwood surrounding the well at the far end. A mile or so over to the west was the river, marking the boundary of Oakman's land; beyond that the rugged mountain terrain began to rise. Once past the mountains then you were into the parched desert region.

Some called this the last valley in America. If he kept riding he'd be in Mexico. But he wasn't going that far; only to one of those splinters of Mexico scattered all over the southwest. Borderlines were for governments, not people; and Sarita, true-blood Mexican down to the tips of her little fingers, had been in Arizona all her life.

He was beyond the parched cotton-woods now, and his heart thudded as he saw the ruins. Such wood as there had been in the making of those simple houses had burned quickly and fiercely when Cuchua's braves had set torches to it. Now the adobe walls were scorched, cracked and crumbling, with desert weed curling up around them.

Ethan suddenly sagged in the saddle, feeling that sense of emptiness and guilt. He guessed it would always be so: a shadow haunting him for the rest of his days. Reining in his horse, he sat staring in a mixture of grief and anger.

He'd known the name of everyone who lived here, had shared their food with them. He'd argued in bad Spanish with the old men; and in that crumbling ruin over there he'd laid curled in a blanket with Sarita and whispered promises he was never to keep.

He swung himself down. That had been the schoolroom over there. Not that they ever spent much time inside. It was too cramped for the numbers who came to learn. And Sarita was always there, helping him to make them understand when his Spanish, or their English, wasn't up to it.

Now some of those eager pupils were dead, others were toiling on the dangerous timber-slopes, others were scratching a miserable living in the *barrio*. In this dark mood Ethan doubted he'd changed things for any of them.

His eyes narrowed as he saw something; a scrap of paper caught amongst the scrub and weeds at his feet. He stooped to pick it up. At the instant he moved his head, from over among the trees round the well a rifle belched lead at him and the slug seared the air only inches above him.

Fragments of the bullet-shattered adobe wall scattered off his hatbrim as he rolled to the ground, bellying himself into some kind of shelter. Ethan drew his gun, and hunched there, watching the alarmed horse canter off. A brittle silence had clamped down, and he stayed still.

From the direction of the well he heard the snicker of a horse. Then, over to his right, he saw movement near to a leaning, weather-pitted wall. Someone was starting to crawl out. The man was well-hidden behind a low rise in the cracked earth; but, as he inched along, now and then his head and shoulders came briefly into sharper view.

After waiting a moment longer, Ethan swiftly knelt up and fired. A revolver wasn't the best weapon for fine shooting but this time he was lucky. The man gave a screech, and reaction brought him yelling to his feet, clutching at his arm just below his shoulder. The second shot caught him square and he went rocketing back into the wall.

Ethan had a moment to ponder the

fact that the man he'd just plugged was a Mexican, when he had to hurl himself flat, as a couple of rifles opened up on him. The rapid, spraying hail of lead sent chunks of the wall down on him. But they wouldn't waste more ammunition than they needed. At least one of them would be cutting round behind him, moving in for the kill while he was pinned down.

There was the briefest of lulls in the volley of shots, as the gunmen paused to reload. Mexicans? He shook his head, baffled. In that sudden silence, he heard a sound; like a boot hitting a stone, or a hammer being cocked. The hairs prickled on his arms, and he tensed, rolling onto his back, swinging the .45 into position.

The man was emerging from behind a wall maybe four yards away. His swarthy face was shadowed by the broad rim of his sombrero, and in any case he had a neckerchief jerked up to the top of his nose. Just his dark eyes showed; blinking fast. And for a moment both men froze. But Ethan froze more. The hammer wouldn't respond to the trigger: there was some fault in his fancy new gun.

He'd fired just two shots and it had jammed itself. It wasn't the moment to curse Zeke Miller, the gunsmith, or himself for not giving the weapon a good try-out.

The eyes above that neckerchief showed puzzlement, then triumph as the Mexican realised what had happened, and Ethan was looking down the muzzle of a Winchester which had a finger tightening inexorably on its trigger.

5

THERE was not even time to hurl his useless weapon at the other man; Ethan knew it was all over for him. And maybe there was a crooked kind of justice in him dying here in the same place where Sarita had died. Except the awaited shot didn't come. The Mexican gave a muffled laugh. "Gun jammed, *señor*?" He took a step forward. "You drop, now. She no good to you no more."

Then he made a mistake he'd never have time to regret. He turned his head a fraction, yelling out in Spanish to the other men, that he had the *gringo* where they wanted him. They were the last words he ever spoke. Maybe, Ethan decided ever after, it was true that your days were numbered in a book somewhere, and he still had a few pages left.

Whatever, he tried the Colt again; the blast and the recoil took him by surprise, but his aim was good and the side of the gunman's head seemed to explode in a sickening spray of blood and bone. He catapulted backwards, and the Winchester fired harmlessly at the sky as he lay twitching for the briefest of moments.

Ethan kept himself low, waiting for the blistering volley of rifle fire from the trees. There was none. He heard the sound of horses riding off in a hurry, and peered up over his bullet-pocked shelter. Two of them, he reckoned, headed east in a dust-billowing panic.

Right now he couldn't begin to think what had spooked them into running. He just slid down, his back muscles sagging against the wall. The smoke he rolled with shaking hands wasted more tobacco than was curled in its paper but it was the best cigarette he'd ever tasted.

Then he heard more horses approaching, and he tensed. Maybe they'd just gone to fetch reinforcements. Scrambling across, he jerked the Winchester from the dead Mexican's stiffening grip.

Once more, he peered over the wall, and his heart seemed to jolt to a stop as he found himself looking into the impassive face of an Apache. At once the Indian jerked away, and waved to the group of riders standing a few yards off. Shakily, Ethan got fully to his feet. He walked a touch unsteadily towards the platoon of US cavalrymen, followed by the Indian, who was plainly an army scout.

The soldiers dismounted. Caked with dust, they looked about as weary as waking men could be. "What in tarnation's been going on here?" demanded the sergeant in charge.

Ethan gave a shrug. "They jumped me. Four, I reckon. Though two, they're deader'n mackerel."

"Four 'gainst one? You're mighty lucky we turned up, then, mister," the sergeant told him. "Hadn't planned on coming this far east. Been on patrol for a week. Just about to head back to our main force when we heard the shooting."

"You looking for Cuchua?"

A soldier laughed. "Only one Injun we're looking for, mister. And his name's Geronimo."

"We'll take a break here," barked the sergeant. "Rest up the horses. Get some coffee brewed quick as you can!"

Ethan led him to the man who'd come up behind him. The sergeant hauled the neckerchief off the shattered face. It wasn't a pretty sight. "Mex, hey? Don't reckon his own ma'd know him. They have something against you?"

Ethan shook his head. "They seemed to be waiting for me, but I didn't tell anyone I was coming."

"Could be they just fancied their chances." The soldier leaned against the wall, pulling a cheroot stub from his stained blouse pocket. "You got a horse, guns. Maybe some money. Life comes cheap out here."

"Don't I know it, sergeant." For the first time Ethan had seen the graves: eight of them over to the left. Clear and smooth mounded, and unmarked.

The sergeant had seen them too. "Friends of yours?"

"I knew this village pretty well," said Ethan softly. "Sure, they were my friends. Good friends." A shiver coursed through him. "Cuchua, the one you're not looking for, cut out from San Carlos. Came calling a few weeks back."

The sergeant rubbed his ear. "I should've known from the burned-out look. When an Apache finishes a place, he finishes it. Ain't heard nothing 'bout this Cuchua, though."

He gave a grim smile. "Then the army don't tell me everything. And don't much signify which Injun did this. Just saw his chance, I guess, like these fellers today."

"Guess it'd make those folk buried under those mounds feel a lot better to know that it was just bad luck that he came calling," snapped Ethan bitterly.

Without waiting for a response from the sergeant he strode over to the burying place. He wondered which was Sarita's resting place. Doubtless Tobe would know. They'd get proper, decent markers up in time.

The sergeant had followed him. "If we come across this Cuchua, he'll pay for this. But we seen no sign of him."

"Could be you're not looking hard enough!"

There was a shout from over by the trees shielding the wellhead. A couple of troopers were leading out a pair of horses, evidently the mounts of the two dead men.

The sergeant stood looking at the graves. "Sorry your friends got kilt, mister. But this here's a big frontier. Can't be everywhere at once."

"Maybe there's not enough of you."

The soldier gave a weary grin. "Apaches, they're like ghosts. Could bring a million men out here, stake out every last yard, and they'd still get by us. And when we do get close they skip across the border. Daresay that's where the mean bastard that done this is now."

"Well let's hope he stays there," muttered Ethan.

"So what you fixing on doing now?"

"Wouldn't turn down a cup of coffee," he replied. "Then I guess I'll get them lashed to their horses and ride them into Chesterville. Let the law take a look at them."

The sergeant fell in step with him. "You got a lawman there? I hear tell that's a pretty wild town."

"There's a sheriff." Ethan scowled. "Though from what I've seen he doesn't fret too much about upholding the law!"

On the way back to Chesterville he stopped off to tell Tobe what had happened. The old man was still half asleep as he stared at the horses' gory baggage. "I ain't never seen either of these bastards before, Ethan. Like that soldier said, they likely jumped you for your horse and gun. Don't 'xactly look like high-class bandits, do they? And these animals ain't much more than walking horse-meat."

"Sag-backed and broken-winded, sure," said Ethan. "But high-class or not, there's still two of them out there somewhere, Tobe. You'd maybe be safer coming back with me."

Tobe yawned. "If trouble's coming, Ethan, it'll come whatever. Only just cleared the din of that heathen place from my ears. Ain't going back till I have to."

"Well, you just watch yourself." Ethan looked at the old man. "You did a good job on those graves, Tobe. Must've been one hell of a job. Ground's pretty stony."

"Man finds strength when he needs to," said Tobe.

"Guess so. Anyhow, soon as I can I'll get some decent markers up. And now I'll get this trash out of your way."

"You do that. I got some serious sleeping to do."

"And snoring, I daresay," he said, as he remounted.

Tobe scowled. "Out here, I can snore as loud as I choose, and nobody to complain! And that's how I like it!"

Ethan sat there, the reins hanging loose. He'd just recalled what Lucinda Oakman had said that morning. "Never get any weird dreams about flying, Tobe? Seeing yourself winging your way through fire'n smoke?"

"What in the name of the Almighty you dribbling about, son? Flying through fire?"

"Don't worry 'bout it," said Ethan, giving the reins a flick. "Just a lot of nonsense. I'll get on and give Sheriff Cutler his present here."

The lawman was none too happy to be given two dead Mexicans. "What in hell's name you bring them back here for?" he blustered, getting twitchy at the crowd gathering round outside his office.

"Don't know who they are, then?"

"I ain't never seen either of 'em." Cutler glared at the crowd, "Anybody here know them?"

There was a shuffling in the crowd, but nobody admitted to knowing the dead men. Cutler shrugged. "Just a couple of no-count bandits. Not even a wanted notice out on them."

"Listen!" Ethan took a step towards him. "These buzzards jumped me. Tried to blow my head off. And you're not showing an ounce of interest in it."

Cutler hauled up his sagging levis. "Outside my juris . . . " He gave up on that word. "Nothing to do with me."

Ethan gave a snort of disgust. "If you were a piece of meat, Cutler, there'd be flies crawling all over you."

"Just get them outa here." Cutler pointed. "Funeral parlour's thataway."

Slowly, Ethan said, "You're telling me that I've got to get these fellers buried?"

"Folk wouldn't want to see their

town taxes wasted on burying a couple of Mexicans." Cutler grinned slyly. "You got a complaint about that, take it up with the mayor."

He turned to his audience, expecting a laugh, and then stepped back, the smug smile fading from his ugly face. The crowd had parted, as three men pushed their way through. Two of them, hulking Mexicans, Ethan recognised as those who'd ordered him out of the *cantina* the other night.

The third man was small, somewhat wiry. He was dressed in dark clothes, narrow neck-tie over frilled shirt, and a low-crowned hat. He pressed the fingertips of his long hands together. "May I take a look, sheriff?"

"What you want, Garcia?" But Cutler was nervous, like a horse when it sensed a rattler nearby. "Sure, take a look, if you've a mind."

Ethan edged aside as Garcia moved to the dead bandits. So this was the man who had the Mexican quarter under his thumb. Certainly not what he'd expected; Garcia had the fastidious bearing of a high-born aristocrat.

One of the bodyguards yanked each head up in turn for Garcia to study the face. After a moment he turned back to the sheriff. There was hardly a trace of an accent in his voice. He had the clipped, fancy way of talking you learned at a fine, expensive school. "I cannot help you, I fear, sheriff. I know neither of these men."

He turned to Ethan. "I will take care of all burial expenses, Mr Winter," he said silkily.

Ethan bristled all of a sudden. This was no Mexican grandee for all his pretty speaking. He was a crook who preyed on human misery. "I guess since they're Mexican, then it may as well be Mex taxes that pays," he snapped.

Garcia gave a slight bow. "I've heard a great deal about you, Mr Winter. Perhaps we could meet sometime, and discuss setting up your school again." Without waiting for a response, he turned to his bodyguards and spoke rapidly in Spanish, and they each led off a horse, with Garcia following them.

Ethan glanced at Cutler. "You seemed kind of twitchy then, sheriff. Who is the bigger man round here? Duke Oakman or Juan Garcia?"

His words were greeted with a cackle of laughter from the crowd, and the sheriff decided to get away from the mockery. "I got work to do!" He stomped back off up the steps into his office, slamming the door.

Ethan took his hired mount back to the livery, then walked back to the hotel. The town was just starting to get into its mood of night-time revelry. He found himself thinking about Garcia. Why would a man like that, educated, fine-spoken, set himself up as the emperor of the squalid, miserable barrio? Surely he could have done a whole lot better for himself.

His thoughts scattered as a couple of saloon girls blocked his way. "A real good deal going at the *Paradise Bar*, cowboy. First drink's free, and if you're special nice to me and Annie then who knows what else you'd get!"

Not more than twenty years old, either of them, still fresh-faced under the rouge. Ethan wondered what had brought them to this. Wondered if there were two grieving mothers somewhere just hoping for their daughters to come home.

This was what Chester had always wanted to avoid in his town. Now it was happening all over: on Main Street, and in the dingy alleys of Mextown, and nobody to put a stop to it. And Oakman and Garcia presiding over it all.

Because he hadn't thrust past them, the girls were emboldened, and one of them pressed herself up against him, running her soft hand down his cheek.

"Maybe you'd like to take a bath, cowboy," she purred seductively. "Always more fun if you have company . . ."

Ethan pushed her off. "Got the

wrong man here, sister."

As he walked on, one of them called, "Don't look like we got any man at all with you, cowboy!"

He was too tired to respond to her shout, and just headed on towards the *Royal* hotel. All he wanted now was to sleep for as many hours as his mind would let him.

The hotel was quieter than when he'd left it. The Mexican women who'd been busy with their brooms and mops had left the air filled with the smell of bleach and soap and polish. The lobby was clean-shabby now, and the haze of dust had been laid for a while.

Cory Boon was lounging in an armchair, reading a newspaper. He looked up, amicably enough, as Ethan walked in. "I was wondering where you'd got to."

"Didn't know you cared!" snapped Ethan.

"Anyway," said the Easterner, folding up his paper. "Wherever you've been, it was probably a lot more restful than this place. Every time I sat down one of those women started cleaning up round me. Chattering noisier than a coop-full of squawking chickens."

Ethan gave an ironic smile. "Sorry to hear that, Mr Boon. A man needs his rest. Still, looks like they did a good job."

Boon shrugged. "I still think Merle's wasting her money. This place'll never come to anything. She'll soon see this violent, coarse kind of life isn't for her."

"Violent, sure," muttered Ethan. "Like while you've been getting inconvenienced by cleaning women, Mr Boon, I've had men trying to kill me."

"What?" Boon gaped incredulously.

"Killed two of them," said Ethan. "But I guess your day's been a whole lot more stressful than mine."

He turned away, and the other man burst out: "You're not serious are you? Just another of your jokes, isn't it?"

"I wish it was, Mr Boon. Wish it was . . . "

As he reached the top of the stairs, Merle Claymore emerged from a door at the end of the corridor. Her petticoats rustled as she walked towards him with a smile. "You're back. You visited the village?" Her eyes were scanning him perceptively. "You've had a tough day, Ethan. Some sort of trouble?"

Not for the first time he wondered why such a good-looking woman had got herself engaged to that whining feller downstairs. He gave an indifferent shrug. "Nothing I couldn't handle. I'll tell you 'bout it, tomorrow. Right now I need some shuteye."

"We've got the boiler working now," she said. "If you feel the need of a hot tub . . . "

He gave a dry laugh, remembering the offer from the saloon girls. "I'll take you up on that tomorrow!"

★ ★ ★

117

It was the same dream he'd had every night since he'd been back here. He was in pitch-darkness, floundering round like a blind man. And Sarita was out there, begging and pleading for him to come to help her. And he knew that whichever way he turned he'd never find her again.

Then he felt a hand on his shoulder; someone shaking him hard. "Ethan, wake up . . . "

He shuddered into wakefulness, feeling the sweat cold on his face. Dawn was just breaking, and in its pale light he saw Micky. "I am sorry to wake you, *amigo*."

Ethan struggled into a sitting position. "Hell, Micky, you were doing me a favour."

"I could not sleep," said the young Mexican. "I know I should have waited till morning, but it would not wait. One of those *hombres* you brought back from my village. I have seen him before."

"You were there in the crowd?"

said Ethan, still waking himself up. "Then you saw Garcia poking his noble nose in?"

Micky's face hardened. "All those manners, it is a mask, Ethan. He is . . . *el malo hombre.*"

"Sure, a wicked man." Ethan rubbed his eyes. "As to the bandit, not surprising you've seen him somewhere, is it?"

"Only once have I seen him," said Micky, still urgent. "He was riding through my village, with another *hombre.*"

"Well, he's riding nowhere any more."

Micky was getting impatient. "You do not listen to me. I was with Sarita. Only a few days before the Apaches come." There was a flash of pain in his dark eyes. "It was the last time I see her. We were sitting by the well . . . talking of you, I think."

"She still talked about me, then?" That rocky lump was in his chest again. "More'n I deserved."

Micky gave an agitated wave of his hand. "Two riders they come by, and for a moment they stop, and stare towards Sarita. They ride on again and I ask her if she know them."

"And one of them was this feller I shot yesterday?" Reaching for his tobacco, Ethan rolled himself a smoke.

Micky nodded. "Sarita she say that she has seen him at the *cantina*. After we lose the land for our horses when Oakman buy it, Sarita she sometimes work there."

"What kind of work was she doing in there?"

"Calm yourself, *amigo*. Sarita she had honour. Her body was not for sale, not like Maria's."

"You talking about that pretty little cousin of yours?"

Micky scowled. "Pretty, *si*. Not so little now. She is Garcia's whore!" His fists clenched. "He preys on our people and she shares his bed when he calls her."

Ethan laid a hand on the young

man's arm. "We're talking about Sarita right now, Micky."

Micky nodded. "She was a fine dancer, my sister. That is why she work at the *cantina*. She was paid less than she was worth, but it helped buy food for the old ones in the village. And she let no man in there lay a finger on her."

He gave Ethan a reproachful look. "Though she did not know if you would return, she was faithful to you, Ethan."

Ethan flinched. "Sure, I know . . . "

"She was going back to the room where the dancers they change their clothes," continued Micky. "This *hombre* was at a table as she passed. He had many dollars, which he is showing to his *amigos*. And Sarita hear him say that he has been paid well for finishing the old *Americano*."

He gave Ethan a long look. "*Señor* Dale had died only two days before this!"

"She thought he was talking about

121

Chester?" exclaimed Ethan. "Sarita must've got it wrong. Chester died of a heart attack! Did she tell anyone else what she'd heard?"

"I do not think so. And she only tell me when she see this *hombre* riding through our village. Months after the old man died. A week later and she is dead also." His face twisted in pain. "Why does my mind tell me it is so important that I wake you and tell you this?"

Ethan stared towards the half-draped window. It was getting lighter all the time as the sun moved higher in the sky. Maybe the man had been talking about a different old *Americano*. He tried that one on Micky.

There was something almost pitying in the young Mexican's face. "How many old ones are there in this town? *Señor* Dale was the only one to die in that week."

"But how do you kill someone so it looks like a heart attack?" Ethan burst out. "And where had this feller got the

122

money from? Who'd hired him?"

Micky shrugged. "It was in Garcia's *cantina*. Garcia is the only one with money in that part of the town."

"Then maybe I'll have to go talk to Juan Garcia." He looked at Micky. "If Chester really was murdered, then I'm as sure as hell going to try do something about it."

6

MERLE stood in the doorway of the hotel kitchen.

"Did you enjoy your bath, Ethan?"

He downed his coffee before answering her. "Helped soak away some of yesterday's aches."

"Micky told me what happened to you yesterday. It seems you're lucky to be alive."

"I guess I am. If those soldiers hadn't come by then I wouldn't be drinking this cup of coffee."

"And Sheriff Cutler refused to do anything?"

"Wouldn't expect otherwise," replied Ethan. "But when it comes to it there's not much even a decent lawman could do about a bunch of bandits. It's a rough country out here."

"So Cory keeps telling me." She

gave a fleeting smile. "He still thinks I should accept Oakman's offer."

Ethan drew his tobacco out. "Don't mind if I . . . "

"You go right ahead." She poured herself a cup of coffee. "You've just proved Cory wrong about nobody out here having any manners at all."

Ethan grinned. "Been in Chicago for two years, remember. Couple of months back here and all the fine ways'll be chipped off me."

"I don't think so," said Merle.

Rolling his smoke, he asked. "Just what did that feller of yours do back in New York?"

"Cory?" She gave an odd little shrug. "I don't believe he's ever done much of anything. His father owned a lot of real estate. Cory used to help in the office. Then there was some scandal or other. Cory's father lost all his money . . . "

He'd raised an amused eyebrow, and Merle bridled defensively. "We'd planned on marrying long before his father went bust, and I became an

125

heiress! You've not seen him at his best so far. He can be kind, thoughtful. Mother adored him. She thought that Cory and I were . . . "

"A match made in heaven?" Ethan suggested.

"Where on earth did you pick up that phrase?"

"Old Pauletta, a woman who lived in the village said it about me and Sarita."

"I wish I'd had a chance to meet Sarita," she said. "Uncle Chester thought the world of her."

"Well, she's gone now. No happy endings there for anyone." He stood up sharply. "Anyhow, I got things to do. Micky's found this feller over the far side of town got a horse for sale. I need myself a good mount."

"You're looking for a horse so you can ride out of here?" Merle stepped a little closer to him. "I was rather hoping that you might stay around for a while."

He shifted uneasily. "I wasn't planning

on cutting out just yet. Few things I want to get sorted out."

As he'd soaked in his bath, he'd pondered what Micky had told him in the dawnlight. Maybe things had been getting out of hand before Chester died, but it was plain that his death had sent them spiralling out of control. On the face of it, if blood-money had been paid over, then it was most likely Garcia who'd done the paying. But it seemed to him that Oakman had benefited most from Chester's death. And that led him to one conclusion: that Garcia and Oakman were in cahoots, both protecting their own vicious interests by helping out the other.

Merle was watching him with a pensive frown, "Get things sorted out? What would those things be, Ethan?"

"This'n that," he returned vaguely. "Now, I'll go find Micky and . . . "

As he moved past her, though, she laid a hand on his arm. "I've been taking a look in Uncle Chester's office. Piles of old papers, bills, receipts. He could never throw anything away. I'd like to show you something interesting."

She led him out into the lobby, and round the counter to the cramped cubbyhole where Chester used to sit, ponderously taking care of his accounts. There was a rattle of footsteps on the stairs, and Cory Boon came into view.

"You're up early, Cory," said Merle wryly.

"Took me hours to get to sleep." He scowled. "The noise from that street. Is there any breakfast?"

"I'll fix you something in a while," she promised. "There's coffee on the stove. Micky's going to find me someone who can do the cooking round here."

"That's excellent news," said Cory sarcastically. "He'll bring in one of his Mexican friends and we'll have to put up with a diet of bacon, beans and chilli."

"I'm sure you'll survive," she responded dryly. "Now go drink some coffee and I'll be with you presently."

He disappeared along into the kitchen, and Merle sighed. "I guess he'll adjust in the end."

Ethan shrugged doubtfully. It didn't seem to him that Cory Boon would ever settle in here, but he said nothing.

"Anyway, take a look at this."

It was laid out on the battered desk; a faded piece of parchment which had been rolled up and which was being held flat by a pile of books at either end. It was a crudely drawn map of the region. There was little detail on it. The river was there, of course, showing the crossing point where some ten years ago Oakman had built the bridge which enabled him to bring his timber from the slopes. The old church was marked, and the site of Sarita's village.

"Have you seen it before?"

"Not as I recall," he replied.

"I think it was drawn by the priest who set up the mission," Merle told him. "There's a name at the bottom: Father Roderigo Jimenez, and a date:

1807. This map was drawn nearly eighty years ago."

He looked closer. "What's that?" There was a small circle drawn roughly on the site where the town now stood, and some tiny, crabbed writing next to it.

"Roughly translated from the Spanish it says something like: 'the place of evil and death'."

A memory was turning cartwheels in Ethan's head: something he'd heard not long ago. He straightened up, trying to fix it clearer. Then it came to him. Something Lizzie, who ran the squalid eating house in the *barrio*, had said. He repeated it to Merle. "In the old times the Indians shunned it as an evil place." He shrugged. "Maybe this priest had heard it from Indians living hereabouts."

"And Uncle Chester never mentioned it?"

He shook his head. "Chester worried about the here and now. He wasn't too concerned with superstition. Tobe might know something about it. Could be it was him found this old paper when he moved into the mission."

"How would this woman know about it?"

He hesitated. "Had some Indian blood in her. Apache grandmother, she said. Lot of folk round here with an Apache squaw in their family tree. Early on there weren't too many white women in this neck of the woods. More than one man found himself an Indian wife."

"Relations between the Indian and the white men must have been rather friendlier in those days."

"Could say," he agreed.

"Maybe this Lizzie would tell me what she knows."

He fired a warning look at the girl. "Don't you go hunting off in the Mexican side of town by yourself. That'd be a fool thing to do. And anyhow, why's it matter?"

"It just shows that this town has a history," said Merle. "One day, when it's a place for decent people, they'll want to know that history."

"You figure they'll be anxious to know it's built on a place of evil and death?"

"You may have a point, there." She removed the books holding the old map down and it rolled itself up obediently. "And I should be worrying more about the future. I've made a start on cleaning things up, and I've plenty of plans, but there's a way to go before I can open up."

"Making a lot of plans is fine and dandy," he said dubiously. "Doesn't mean they'll come true." But he managed a grin. "But I sure wish you luck. Now, I'll get about my own business."

Micky was outside, watching what was going on in the street. There was an odd, wistful look in his eyes.

"You hankering after your pitch on the bank steps?"

"It was not all bad," retorted the young Mexican.

"And you've got a better job now," Ethan reminded him.

"*Si*, but for how long?" Micky spread his hands. "The *señorita* she has a dream. But look at this place, Ethan. A nest of cut-throats and robbers; men passing through. They do not need such a hotel as she plans."

"You sound like that streak of misery she's set on marrying," said Ethan. "Now quit fretting. Merle's not giving up her dream that easily. Come on, we gotta see a man about a horse. On the edge of town, you said?"

"*Si*, a few acres of land. He grows vegetables, sells to the eating houses . . . " He hesitated. "You have said nothing to the *señorita* about what Sarita told me?"

"Hell, no. I'd like to ask Tobe Wellbeloved what he thinks. Never gave any hint that he thought Chester's death was suspicious, but it'd be worth talking to him." He gave a shake of his head, "Now let's stop jawing about this for a while, Micky. You say this feller's a farmer? Not trying to land me with a beast that's been pulling a plough, are you?"

"This horse pull a plough?" The young man's eyes lit up. "Never. He is an emperor among horses. If I could still ride, then it is such a horse I would choose for myself."

"Must be pretty good then," commented Ethan. "If you know anything, you know your horseflesh, Micky."

Micky nodded. "I never rode a horse I could not tame. And all I ever suffered was a few bruises." He winced, "It took the timber slopes to finish my riding days."

"And maybe one day Oakman'll pay for that."

The young Mexican gave him a thoughtful sideways glance. "You have plans for Oakman?"

"Let's just say that both Oakman and Garcia need slicing down to size. I'd kind of like to be the one who does the slicing."

"You must take care," Micky counselled. "Unbroken horses they are dangerous, but they carry no guns."

"How much do you know about Garcia?"

Micky shrugged. "He is like the spider, trapping all who come near in his web."

"How long's he been here in Chesterville?"

"A year, a year and half a year, maybe."

Ethan sniffed, "And nobody knows anything about him?"

"Old Pauletta she got some crazy idea that she has seen him before."

Coming to a sudden stop, Ethan stared. "Pauletta? From the village? I was only just talking about her to Merle this morning. I figured she must have died in the attack."

"No. She moved to town to live with the son of her son. He say he look after her. Things they get very hard in the village, at the end. Now he has died, and she is alone. Not a good place,

Ethan. There are rats . . . "

Ethan could see that wrinkled old face in his mind's eye now. Pauletta had lived in the village longer than anyone. Her memories went back to a time long before Chesterville existed. The villagers had respected, loved her, for all her fierce, crabby ways. Naturally Pauletta had to meet Ethan before he could set up the school. Had to give her verdict on him.

"Living by herself?" Ethan cut in. "Hell, Micky, she must be over eighty, nearer ninety maybe. I reckon if you talk to Merle, she'll do something to help the old lady."

"*Si*, I was thinking I must do this. She is very proud, though. Maybe she not come."

"You tell her that if she won't come of her own accord, then I'll hoist her out of that rat-hole over my shoulders." He grinned, "But what's this about her recognising Garcia?"

Micky gave a faint smile. "She is old. A little crazy sometime. She say she has seen him long ago, when she was much younger. That he has sold his soul to the devil so he may stay young for ever."

"Maybe she's right," muttered Ethan. "Anyhow, you talk to Merle about that old hen, Micky, you hear."

They walked on a little while longer beyond the edge of town, and then Micky pointed. "Now we are here."

Ethan spotted the horse at once; grazing in a rough-built corral behind the barn which stood next to a tumbledown shack. He let out a long whistle. The stallion was ebony black; and even from here he could sense the power rippling through its muscles.

He began to move towards the corral, and then the farmer appeared; a rail-thin oldster with a tobacco yellowed moustache. There was an uneasy expression on his face.

"A real fine looking animal," said Ethan. "How come you own a horse like that, mister?"

The old man hesitated. "Was my

boy's mount," he said. "Bred him up from a foal."

"How come he's selling him?"

"Boy's dead," came the terse response. "Got himself shot in a brawl in the *Paradise* a few weeks back."

"Sorry to hear that." The old feller had spoken evenly enough, but there was pain in his eyes. Came hard when a man lost his son. "So what's your price, mister?"

The old-timer shook his head. "He's sold already."

Micky glared angrily, "You told me you would not sell until my *amigo* had seen him."

"Calm down, Micky." Ethan faced the old man. "I'll better any price you've been offered."

There was a wagon-sheet pallor on the wrinkled face. "Couldn't take it, mister. Duke Oakman's taking him instead of the dues I owe."

"Well if I pay you," persisted Ethan, "then you can give him his dues in bills instead of horseflesh."

"Can't do that." The old man looked twitchier than ever. "Had a visit from one of Oakman's hands after this young feller came to look at the horse . . . "

"Name of Hicks?" The old-timer nodded. "And he said that selling to me'd bring a lot of trouble your way?"

The farmer stepped forward. There was a pleading light in his old eyes now. "Listen, mister, I'd like to sell to you. But it's tough enough making a living without getting the wrong side of Duke Oakman. He'd make sure nobody'd buy any of my produce off me. You see how it is?"

"I see fine." Ethan scowled. It was a childish kind of trick to pull. But then Oakman had that kind of nature.

The old man eyed him nervously. "It ain't the only horse in town, mister."

"Maybe not." Ethan cast a glance towards the corral. "But it's the one I want. I'll maybe have words with Duke Oakman about this. I'll be back."

"Just don't cause any trouble for me, mister, please."

"I promise you that." Ethan studied him thoughtfully. "You grow good vegetables?"

"Best round here." A note of pride entered that quavering voice. "Real tasty."

"Well, you just keep growing them," said Ethan firmly. "You'll soon have somewhere else to sell them. When the *Royal* hotel gets going it'll take everything you can grow."

"Maybe," said the farmer doubtfully. "Though I hear tell Duke Oakman's not too happy about that place opening up again. Could be he'll find a way of stopping that."

"That's not your worry. Come on, Micky, let's get back to the hotel. I've got some thinking to do."

They headed back. Underneath, Ethan seethed with resentment about Oakman. But he was determined to keep his anger in check. He didn't want that horse so badly that he was about to do something dumb and get killed for it.

"There is something happening at the hotel!" Ethan had been striding along, taking no notice of his surroundings, but Micky's urgent voice cut into his thoughts, and now he saw that a crowd was gathering outside the hotel.

A moment later and the crowd scattered. A cheer went up as there was the sound of smashing glass and one of the lobby armchairs came sailing through the window at the front. It was rapidly followed by a table which splintered as it crashed to the ground.

Ethan put on speed now, and shouldered his way roughly through the gawping spectators. He got inside to a scene of destruction. There looked to be half a dozen of them in there, one man wielding a sledgehammer as he set about demolishing the hotel counter.

They were Triple-O men, no doubt of that: big, burly and ugly. He recognised the man with the hammer as one of those who'd been tormenting Charley Lo the other day. With his arrival, silence fell on the lobby. For a moment there was no sound in that intense hush save the hoarse, jerky rasp of someone's breathing.

And then Merle let out a cry. "Ethan! Watch out!"

She was over at the far side of the lobby, being held down in a chair by a grinning Curly Hicks. Rage seared in Ethan, and his hand went for his gun. At the same moment, though, someone came at him from behind, and a boot lashed viciously at his shins, sending him stumbling forward.

He regained his balance in time to twist round, and duck the oncoming blow. It was a wild swing, unbalancing his assailant, and Ethan took the chance to lay a blistering punch on the exposed jaw. There was a sound like a hatchet sinking into a chopping block, and the yowling man careered away clutching his broken jaw.

Two more came at him now, and Ethan wasn't quick enough to dodge one of the flailing blows, taking it in the ribs. He buckled slightly, and a second punch sailed over his head. A moment later and he whipped in a savage right which brought a spraying gush of blood from a split lip. Then he stopped another charging attacker with a lifted knee which crunched into the tender area just below the belt.

As the winded man sagged Ethan flattened his nose with a piledriving punch. The rest of them seemed reluctant to come deal with him just for the moment. He took the opportunity to swing round and crash his way through the debris of splintered chairs and tables and get to where Curly Hicks still stood.

Hicks grunted as Ethan yanked him away from Merle by his shirt-front, but almost in the same instant he lunged forward butting with his bony head, and opened a cut under Ethan's eye. He was jerking back when Ethan got an arm round his head, hugging him to stop him butting again.

They both lost balance, and crashed

to the floor, rolling over and over, cursing wildly as they tried unsuccessfully to lay punches on each other. It was Hicks's misfortune that the man with the sledgehammer chose to join in the tussle now. He towered over the grappling pair and heaved a kick at Ethan's face.

Unluckily for Curly Hicks he chose that moment to jab a punch at Ethan. The sunburst rowel of his crony's spur carved through Curly's shirt sleeve, splitting his forearm open from elbow to wrist. Curly gave an animal squeal of anger and pain, and scrabbled away as the ugly gash spouted a scarlet fountain.

Breathless, and with blood dribbling from the cut under his eye, Ethan pushed himself to his feet. His gun was in his hand now, and Oakman's men cowered back as he swung it round to each of them in turn. "I've got a slug for each of you," he barked. "And it wouldn't take much to make me pull this trigger. Just you get out of here, and take this trash with you . . . " he flicked the muzzle towards the moaning Curly, "before he paints the whole floor red."

Micky was standing in the doorway now, and he eased himself to one side as the men took themselves out to an ironic cheer from the audience out in the street.

For his part Ethan grabbed at one of the more undamaged chairs, setting it on its legs, and slumped down.

Shakily Merle came over to him. "I've never seen anything like it," she said. "You took on six of them."

"I was lucky," he said.

"What's been going on here?" Cory Boon came in, staring aghast at the wreckage around him. He moved swiftly to Merle. "Are you all right?"

She looked at him narrow-eyed. "Where were you Cory?"

He bristled. "What do you mean? I told you, I had some business in the bank."

"You missed a real party, Mr Boon,"

said Ethan. "Surprised the noise didn't reach you over there."

"We did hear something, but Mr Shelby said that kind of commotion was only too common in this town." He broke off. "Who did all this?"

"I presume they were Mr Oakman's hired hands," answered Merle. "And if Ethan hadn't turned up the Lord knows what might have happened to me."

Cory rested a hand on her arm, and Ethan couldn't help noticing how she moved away from his touch. "I guess we've got to be grateful to you then, Winter."

Merle turned to Ethan. "Surely the sheriff will have to do something about this?"

Micky hobbled across. "He will do nothing against Oakman, *Señorita* Claymore."

"Can't you see all this is impossible, Merle?" said Cory. "If you repair all the damage they'll only come back." He stared at Ethan. "Tell her, Winter.

This is no place for her. You might not be here next time they come calling."

Gingerly Ethan touched the cut under his eye. It seemed to have stopped bleeding. He was sceptical about Cory's late arrival, though he doubted the man would have been much of an ally. But there was some truth in what he was saying.

"Maybe Oakman will get his come-uppance one day," he said to Merle. "But I was lucky today. If there'd been more of them, could all have been different."

Hands on hips, she fixed him with her grey eyes. Her coiled-up hair was coming loose. She didn't make quite cool a picture as normal but she didn't look scared, either.

"A war's never won with the first battle," she declared. "Didn't Uncle Chester ever tell you that?"

"May've said something of that kind," Ethan conceded.

"Maybe those men did me a favour.

These chairs and tables weren't worth anything. And I was thinking of changing the window glass, too." Her face lit up with a smile. "I'm not beaten yet!"

7

MR SHELBY the bank president squirmed edgily under Ethan's gaze. "I'd help you if I could, Mr Winter."

"If Oakman can hold a town meeting, then so can decent, honest folk," said Ethan. "And if you're there, then maybe those folk'll come out of the shadows and . . . "

The middle-aged man shook his head fiercely. "Can't be done, Mr Winter. Least, not by me."

"When I came in here a few days back," Ethan reminded him, "I reckoned you were looking to the day when this town got back on the rails. Miss Claymore got her hotel smashed up yesterday. She's not running away."

Shelby gave him a troubled look. "I had her fiancé in here yesterday. He was asking me if I'd try helping him persuade her to give up the notion."

Ethan glared. "Never had you written down as a coward, Mr Shelby. Chester told me of the time there was a hold-up here. You killed one of the gang, and took two prisoners."

A momentary flash of pride at the memory showed itself in the banker's eyes, but it swiftly faded. "I was a lot younger then, Mr Winter. And this is different. Duke Oakman's my biggest depositor . . . "

"And I daresay Garcia likes things the way they are too," snapped Ethan. "You sending hardworking Mexicans back into his clutches. Maybe I should get the folk in the *barrio* to join me. And then maybe you'd have something else to be scared about, Mr Shelby!"

"It'll do no good threatening me, Mr Winter."

"No," growled Ethan. "Someone else got there first!" He stood up. "I'll tell you one thing, though, Mr Shelby. You can talk as silver-tongued as you like but you won't persuade Merle Claymore into quitting."

"Then maybe you should try," said Shelby dully. "Suppose they start on her? You can't be around every hour of the day. I fear you'll find precious few allies in Chesterville. Only wish it were different."

"I need some fresh air!" Storming out of the office, he glowered at the bank teller. "How do you feel about joining up with me to try and break Oakman's hold on this town?"

Leeker gave a nervous laugh. "I got a wife and two children, mister. I'd be crazy to take a risk like that."

And that, Ethan knew, was how most would see it. This was a town ruled by fear. Oakman and Garcia, two sides of the same coin. Not only would a lot of the more respectable folk be scared, many of them would be doing quite nicely out of this roistering town. Money, wickedly come by or not, shouted louder than a fairground roustabout.

He walked back to the hotel. It was a dismal place right now. They'd boarded up the smashed windows, and cleared the rest of the debris. But once the panes were replaced, and new furniture brought in, there'd be little to stop Curly Hicks and his crew starting over.

"Anybody here?" His voice echoed round the emptiness.

"Only me." Merle Claymore came out of the kitchen.

"Where's Micky and Cory, then?"

"As to Cory," replied Merle with a shrug, "I couldn't say. He was rather sullen this morning."

"Still trying to make you see sense?"

"As far as I'm concerned," said Merle a touch frostily, "Cory is butting his head against a barn door on that subject. Oakman doesn't own this town, and he certainly isn't going to terrorise me out of my inheritance."

"Maybe. But he's got a lot more men than you have, Merle." He looked at that perfect unblemished complexion, and a shiver went through him as he thought of Shelby's warning. He'd been battered around as much as most in his years out west. Another scar now and then made little difference to him. But on Merle Claymore's beautiful face it would be close to being a blasphemy.

She seemed to understand what was going through his head. "So you've started to think I should give in to Oakman, have you?"

"Not exactly that," he replied uneasily.

"It'd be difficult for you to stand guard on me twenty-four hours a day," she said. "And I'm not expecting that. But there is someone else who could help."

"In this town?" He shook his head. "Forget it."

"The man who built the hotel," she said. "You know it was the first building to go up in Chesterville."

"Sure, I know that. On the site of the old trading post. But I'm not so sure Tobe's got a lot of interest in it now." Ethan smiled faintly. "But I guess if you could sweet-talk him into joining up with us for a while, well, it'd even up the odds some."

"And that's exactly what I plan to do, Ethan. I was intending to take myself out to his place this morning."

"Take yourself?" Ethan's eyes narrowed. "Where's Micky got to, then?"

"I've sent him off to see Pauletta."

"Oh, he told you about her?"

"I'd heard of her, of course. Uncle Chester wrote long letters. I sometimes felt I knew people here better than those at home."

"Like Cory for instance?" he suggested dryly.

Merle ignored that. "Anyway, an old lady like that shouldn't be living the way she is, in a crumbling shack, infested by rats. I've told Micky he must bring her here."

"This mightn't be the safest place for her right now." He shrugged. "But can't be worse than where she is."

"Anyway with Micky visiting her, I

have no driver presently. I can handle a pair of horses myself, but . . . "

"I'll take you out to Tobe's," Ethan butted in swiftly. "Can't say I like driving a buggy, but till I can get my hands on that farmer's stallion I got no horse. Let's go see what the Preacher's got to say."

★ ★ ★

There was no sign of Tobe in the low adobe shack next to the ruined church. It was dark inside, with all the shutters closed. Ethan unhooked one pair, and let a little light in.

"Where do you think he's got to?" asked Merle nervously, looking round the sparsely furnished room.

"Don't worry about Tobe, he's a survivor." He looked towards where Tobe hung his old Spencer rifle. "Anyhow, he's taken his gun with him. Gone hunting, I daresay."

"Do you think there's any point in waiting?" Walking over to an old rocking chair, next to a low trestle bed, Merle sat herself down.

"Couldn't say."

There was a book lying atop the tangled blanket on the bed. Merle picked it up, flicking the pages. "Edgar Allan Poe. Have you ever read these stories, Ethan?"

"Sure. Used to carry them in my saddle-pack. That feller had a twisted kind of imagination."

Merle nodded. "Mother found me reading a book of his once, and snatched it off me. Said it'd give me nightmares."

Ethan grinned, "So you went ahead and read it anyway?"

"Of course. How did you know?"

"Seems to me," he said, "when someone tries to stop you doing a thing, you get even more fixed on doing it."

Merle fixed him with her grey eyes. "That's not a bad thing, is it?"

"Depends," he said, feeling uncomfortable under that frank scrutiny.

"Still," she recalled, "Mother was right. I did have nightmares. Especially about one particular story. 'The Tell-Tale Heart' it's called."

"I know it. About this feller who murders an old man for his money and then cuts him up and buries him under the cabin floor."

"And then starts hearing the sound of the old man's heart beating until he goes mad and confesses the murder." Merle stood up closing the book sharply, and dropping it on the bed. "I think I'd go mad living in such a lonely place."

"Well, Tobe's got his funny ways," said Ethan. "But I don't reckon you could call him mad." He watched her walk over to a long table at the other side of the room; piled with a jumble of things; cooking pots, plates, jars of beans and the like.

"He seems to have so few possessions." Then she let out a cry of surprise. "But he has one of these!" She turned, holding a small brass-bound spyglass. "Mother had one of these. Uncle Chester gave it to her."

There was an excited, girlish look in her eyes. "I used to go up onto the top floor of our house and stare out of it for hours, watching people going by in the street."

"See anything you shouldn't have seen?"

"Oh, I'm scarce going to tell you that until I know you better, Ethan Winter," she said coquettishly.

"Well, there's nothing to see out there," he said. "Now I guess we should get back to town."

She set the little telescope back on the table. "If it wouldn't be too painful for you, Ethan, then perhaps we could go and see the village."

He stiffened. "Seems to me that you're looking for trouble every which way you turn."

"Those bandits are hardly likely to still be there," she observed lightly. "Lightning never strikes twice in the same place."

"I've never been too sure about that saying. How's anybody know that for sure?"

"Anyway, this time you'll be on your guard. And another thing . . . " She darted back to the table. "We'll borrow Tobe's spyglass. If anyone's lurking around there we'll be able to see them a long way off."

It suddenly came to him that she was seeing this as a kind of exciting game. Sure, it was easy to get infected by her enthusiasm. There was a fierce determination in her to win out against all obstacles; just as there had been in her Uncle Chester. Sometimes, though, stubbornness could be close on foolhardiness. And in a lot of ways Merle Claymore was kind of innocent in the ways of this tough, rough world.

He suddenly caught himself recollecting a woman he'd met once. A big woman in a faded calico dress living in an isolated cabin along with a herd of children. She'd had the expressionless face of all pioneer women. Her husband had died somewhere along the line, and she was just about surviving. Probably she had never known anything but sorrow and disappointment and hardship and she was stoically facing a future that would hold more of the same.

Merle had never known that kind of hardship. He felt she was still underestimating the problems she had to face. Could she really survive the worst of what this territory could throw at her? Maybe Cory, and Mr Shelby, were right, and she'd be better back in New York, among places and people she knew.

"Come on, Ethan," she urged. "If you don't take me then I'll only end up going out there by myself. And you wouldn't want that, would you?"

"I guess not," he said in a low voice. Her face was very close to his; he could smell the sweetness of her perfume. Maybe it'd do her good to see what had happened to Sarita's village. Show her that not everyone out here was a winner, however hard they fought back.

He gave a nod, and cleared his throat. "Well, you just keep that spyglass close to you. And if I get even the smallest feeling that something at the village isn't quite right, then we're riding straight back to town, pronto. And no argument."

"No argument," she agreed sweetly. "Thank you, Ethan."

As they headed out from Tobe's place, and down the rocky trail to the village, Merle said, "This man Garcia, the one who runs things in the Mexican quarter . . . "

"What about him?"

"Do you know anything about him?"

"No more'n you do, I daresay," he said. "When there's a place where people are bowed down by misery there's always someone ready to take the chance to make things even more miserable for them."

"But where did he come from? And

how did he manage to take over?"

He twitched the reins, and the horses speeded up a little. "Old Pauletta reckons he's signed his soul to the devil," he said. "So he can stay young for ever."

"What are you talking about?" she exclaimed.

"Something Micky told me yesterday," he replied. "And in a town built on a place of evil and death, maybe that's just as likely as anything else."

"Isn't he more likely to be in league with Duke Oakman than with Satan?"

He glanced at her, with a curling smile. "I see you've been doing a lot of thinking, too."

"It's obvious, isn't it?" Merle said. "As long as Chesterville stays wild and untamed, nobody's going to try and clean things up in the Mexican quarter. And with Garcia keeping his power over the Mexican population, Oakman doesn't have to worry about them."

She flicked at a strand of hair come

loose from under her bonnet. "It also seems to me that Uncle Chester's death was a boon to both of them." She frowned. "It was a real shock when he died. He was a lot older than mother, but I think she always thought her brother would live for ever."

Ethan felt his hands tighten on the reins. Was this the time to tell her what Micky had told him? About Sarita's suspicions that Chester hadn't died a natural death?

But he had other things on his mind now; the village was coming in sight as the buggy crested a rocky rise. "You just take a look through Tobe's spyglass. Looks quiet and deserted enough, but it did the last time I came by here."

She raised the small telescope to her eye, twisting its barrel to focus it. He glanced at her, "See anything?"

She peered a moment longer, then lowered the spyglass, shaking her head. "Not a thing. As you say it looks quiet as the grave . . . " She let out a breath. "I'm sorry, Ethan. That was a bad choice of words."

"Bad, but true," he said. "Used to be such a bustling, cheerful place. 'Specially when they were doing well with the horse-breeding. Now look at it. A ghost town getting strangled by scrub and weeds. Couple more years and there'll be less than nothing left."

"You think it's died for ever? Micky told me there was a good well there."

"The memory of the blood that was spilled there's going to be a lot more powerful than the draw of a water supply. Won't be the first village or town to die." He looked at her again. "Just take another peek through that glass."

"There's nothing."

"No, I guess not." Maybe that faint prickling on the back of his neck was out of memory of what had happened rather than any sixth sense of what might be waiting today.

A few minutes more and they were into the devastated village. As he'd hoped, it did quieten down his companion as she looked at the scorched timbers, and no doubt tried to imagine what it had been like on that last night.

In a low voice, she said, "Aren't you going to stop?"

"We'll just wheel through," he said. "And go round that stand of trees by the well."

"Whatever for?"

"Just like to take a look from every side. First sound and these horses get whipped into a gallop."

Not that there was any sound, apart from the hooves on the sun-baked trail, and the buggy's creaking. They were almost at the trees now, and he felt himself relaxing as much as any man could in this place haunted by its bloody memories. Merle had twisted round, and was looking at the line of graves. "Eight of them," she murmured.

"And I guess there'd have been nine if Pauletta hadn't gone to live with her grandson. And maybe even an old woman of ninety'd find living among rats preferable to being under one of those mounds."

"Life always being better than death?"

"Mostly," he grunted.

She started to move back in her seat, facing front, and then she let out a scream. Like a shadow from hell an Apache had appeared from the cover of a tumbled shack, launching himself at the buggy. He got an arm round the screaming girl and pulled her sideways down to the ground.

Grabbing for his side-arm, Ethan spat out a blistering oath; cursing himself for being so dumb as to come back here again so soon. But it was too late. The buggy swayed as another Indian leapt up on the back, and caught Ethan in a vicious neck lock, heaving him off his seat.

With a razor-edged knife hovering less than an inch from his throat, he didn't struggle. One twitch of that swarthy wrist and his life would gurgle redly away. The rig stopped as the horses were reined back. The knife moved away from his throat, and Ethan was hauled down, and shoved over to the trees, to where a tearstained Merle crouched, hunched up in terror of the half circle of stonily watching Indians.

"It's all my fault, Ethan," she moaned. "I couldn't see anything through the spyglass: the lens was broken."

Through gritted teeth, he hissed, "But you were so set on coming you didn't say anything."

Not, he knew, that she would have seen anything, even if the telescope had been unbroken, and three times as powerful. If an Apache wanted to stay hidden, you could walk over him and not see him. He started to put his arm round Merle, to try and calm her down, but one of the watching Indians gave a warning grunt, and pulled his knife from out of his belt.

Ethan shifted away from her again, leaning back against the tree. There wasn't a lot he could do, except just sit tight and pray for the impossible. Which was that these fellers meant him and his companion no harm, and would let them go unscathed. He wondered what they were waiting for. It gave him time to take them in, though.

For all their ferocious expressions, they were just a bunch of youngsters. Skinny, even half-starving. Not stripped down to their breechclouts for battle action. They were wearing a weird assortment of gear. One or two had on Mexican uniform blouses, gold-braid and buttons. One was sporting a beat-up cavalry forage cap. Another was wearing what looked like a woman's dress, ripped off at the knees.

They were poorly-armed too. Only one rifle between them, and that was an ancient muzzle-loader. "Why are they just standing there?" said Merle in a strangled whisper.

"I'd ask them," he said, "'cept I don't speak Apache."

Then all of a sudden one of them did make a move. Taller than the others, with a recently-healed scar streaking down the side of his face from cheekbone to chin, he stepped forward, and heaved Merle to her feet. She froze in terror as the Apache ran his hands down her shoulders and over her breasts.

"Now you just leave her . . . " Ethan was on his feet; the bile of anger boiling in him. Was this how they'd treated Sarita? He felt a painful tautness in the cords of his neck, and sweat threw its spreading stains across his shirt. The girl's tormentor carried on with his pawing, watched impassively by his comrades, and then, without warning he yanked at her blouse, half ripping it from her.

Ethan could take it no longer. He thrust himself away from the tree, taking them all by surprise. He was upon the tall Indian in an instant, pulling him round. The Apache gaped at him, wide open to Ethan's punch which sledged him squarely on his chin, dropping him like a stone into a lake.

A moment later and Ethan was pinned down viciously, flat on his back, his arms stretched out. He could hear Merle sobbing softly over to his left, and he knew now that this was the end. His own shirt was torn open, and a brave crouched beside him, holding a large, slightly curved knife which glinted in the metallic glare of the sun.

Ethan swallowed hard; he knew that kind of blade too well to fool himself that he could expect one swift, merciful finishing blow. His mind went back to his early days out West, to the buffalo hunters he'd seen out on the plains. They'd used knives like that. Sharp enough to take the hide off a dead buffalo, or the skin from a living man!

8

"YOU can't do this to him, you savages!"

Twisting his head slightly, Ethan saw Merle standing up. Her blouse was half falling off her, she'd lost her bonnet, and her hair was hanging loose. He felt sick with remorse at having agreed to bring her here. Lightning didn't strike twice, she'd said. Well, she'd been wrong about that.

"Just stay still!" he yelled, and then a swarthy hand clamped over his mouth.

The Apache he'd felled had been squatting near him, like the others, but now Merle had reminded him of her existence. He headed for her now, and the skinning knife was drawn away from Ethan's chest.

From the way that scar-faced Indian had grabbed the terrified girl, there was no mistaking his intentions. Ethan felt like his throat was filled with jumping cactus spikes. He'd always doubted the common view that imagining something was never as bad as the reality of it. Pain was pain. There were all kinds of torture though, and watching another's agony and degradation, especially Merle's, was one of the worst he could think of.

She screamed, "You get off me, you brute!" He hurled her to the ground, and she lay half on her side, bruised by the fall, sobbing, and doubtless praying too. Why the hell had the Apaches decided to return here?

Maybe it was his own punishment for abandoning Sarita. Tobe often said, in that gloomy biblical way he had, that men always reaped the harvest they'd sown. But it wasn't right for Merle to be punished for what he'd done.

He longed to close his eyes, but he couldn't shut his ears. Anyhow, his eyes would be forced open again, one way or another. They'd make him watch and listen to every detail of what they were doing to the white woman, until he'd be pleading for them to kill her. And when she was dead, then they'd begin on him and it'd be his turn to be begging for the relief of death.

Then one of the watching Apaches gave a guttural shout of alarm, pointing northwards. Ethan tried to move his head to see what the Indian had seen, but he was kept pinned down. They were talking agitatedly amongst themselves, and suddenly he was no longer being held down. He looked for Merle, and saw that she'd scrabbled back to one of the trees, pressing herself against it, as if hoping the trunk would swallow her up and take her away from this nightmare.

A single horse was coming, riding fast, hooves drumming on the baked earth. The Indians' ferocity had abated, and they were waiting nervously. Ethan, conscious he might be taking his life in his hands, sat up, rubbing his bruised arms. But they all ignored him. Now he saw the rider; only fifty yards away, and closing fast. His heart sank into his boots as he saw it was another Apache, his long hair streaming as he rode furiously towards the trees.

The pony careered up, and its rider swung himself down even before it had stopped, landing cat-like on moccasined feet. Instinctively, Ethan knew this must be Cuchua. There was an air of authority about this bronze-muscled young man. For a moment he just stood there motionless, arms folded across his bare chest. His dark eyes flickered to where Merle crouched, rested on Ethan momentarily, and then he turned to the tall, scarred Indian. He took two steps forward and suddenly lashed him across the face with the back of his hand.

Scar-face barely winced. The two exchanged words. Cuchua was angry, the other Indian was speaking softer, his hands moving expressively like a man justifying his actions. It didn't stop Cuchua's rage though, and he turned on the other braves, who looked for all the world like schoolboys getting a whipping from their teacher's tongue.

It seemed to Ethan that the world had been turned downside up. He knew a few words of Apache, but not near enough to get any clue what was happening. Maybe Cuchua was telling them that they should have waited for him. Maybe this was just a temporary release, and soon there'd be the smell of fear here again, and the certain promise of long shrieking hours of writhing pain.

Cuchua thrust Scar-face aside and now with long strides walked up to Ethan. He reached down a hand. Ethan hesitated. This was the man he'd vowed to kill; the man whose evil deeds had haunted his nightmares. The bastard who'd taken Sarita from him.

Yet he reached up and allowed Cuchua to pull him to his feet. They stood face to face, and then the Indian spat on the ground between them. Ethan tensed. Cuchua raised his head, and laid a hand across his chest.

He spoke in English, haltingly, but clear enough. "They should not have done this to you, or the white woman."

Merle croaked hoarsely, "Ethan, what's happening?"

Standing his ground, Ethan held the gaze with the Indian. "Seems we're not to be skinned alive, just yet," he said. "You come over here, Merle, and stand by me."

She stumbled across, and he put his arm round her shoulder, pulling him close to her. "You'll be the one they call Cuchua, I guess?"

"You have heard my name?"

"I heard what you done here!"

"Don't antagonise him, Ethan," Merle hissed fearfully.

"What does the white woman say?"

"She's telling me not to rile you." Maybe it was dangerous talking to Cuchua like this. But he knew enough about Apaches to know that begging for your life never did any good. A frightened man was treated with contempt; no better in their eyes than a skulking cur-dog.

"You believe that my people did this?" He swept his arm round, covering the village in one gesture.

"Your boys have just been showing us a little of what they can do."

Cuchua turned and spoke to one of the watching Indians, who stepped across, and handed him a bulging hide pouch. A moment later and Cuchua untied the neck of the pouch and there was a clinking clatter as he tipped out its contents. Thirty, maybe forty, cartridge shells. The Apache stooped and picked one up, thrusting it towards him. "You know guns, white man?"

Ethan frowned uneasily. "Sure. I'd say this here's been ejected from a Winchester repeater."

"There are many such shells fallen in this place. We have no rifles such as these. We were not here when the village burned." He pointed. "We were hunting game in the south-country."

Ethan shrugged. "As to these shell-cases," he said, "I had a chunk of trouble here a day or so back. Bandits. They had Winchesters." He gave an uncertain shake of his head, though. Sure, they'd opened up on him furiously that day; but not enough to account for all this spent ammunition.

Cuchua was watching him wordlessly, arms folded across his chest. Merle hugged closer to Ethan. "Just agree with him Ethan. If he says he didn't attack the village . . . "

"Apaches were seen heading this way on that night," Ethan flared out. "An old man close to dying gabbed out your name, Cuchua. You saying he was lying?"

"There is a yellow-leg at the San Carlos," said Cuchua slowly, "who can hold a coin in his hand . . . " He held out his own hand, palm up, "Then close his fingers so, and make the coin disappear." He flicked a finger at his ear, "And then he can seem to pull the coin from another man's ear."

"That's real interesting," retorted Ethan.

"There is no magic in it," continued Cuchua. "He make those who watch believe they have seen what they have seen."

"Well, all this was no conjuring trick," Ethan blasted back. "There's eight graves there. And there's dead people buried in them."

"My braves did not kill them. When this happened we were far away. We were hunting in the south-country. Chilli Woman has told me what stories have been told of the killing at this place."

"Chilli Woman? Who the hell . . . ?" Then Ethan stared incredulously. "You talking about Lizzie, who runs the eating house?"

"Chilli Woman has been a good friend to my people on the agency. She brings food, medicine for the sick children. She has good Apache blood in her veins."

"Sure," returned Ethan, "I know she does. Are you telling me that you've just been into Chesterville?"

Unexpectedly, Cuchua gave a low chuckle. "White man cannot tell one Apache from another. There are many who share Apache blood in that place. I was not known by any who saw me."

Ethan recalled the half-breeds he'd seen on his visit into the *barrio*, and nodded. "You're saying that you only just found out from Lizzie about what happened here?"

A flickering expression unusually close to impatience crossed Cuchua's face. "I need no telling. I know truth of what happened in this place!"

"You saying it was another bunch of Apaches?" asked Ethan. "Geronimo, maybe?"

There was a mutter of conversation from the watching Indians as they recognised the war-chiefs name being spoken. "Not Geronimo," said Cuchua. He spat on the ground again. "Not any Apache. But men who disguised themselves as my people and rode upon this place."

Merle suddenly sagged. "Ethan, I

can't take much more of this. Is any of what he's saying true?"

"Sit," said the Indian suddenly. "The white woman is weary. Sit, and I tell you how I know these things."

"And why should you want to tell me?"

Cuchua stared at him for a long moment. "You are the one Chilli Woman spoke of, I think. The *Americano* who has blood in his veins and not water."

"Lizzie mentioned me?" Ethan shifted uneasily. "Hell, I only met her the once."

A little flash of spirit returned to Merle. "You evidently made a good impression, Ethan."

"She saw in your eyes that truth is more to you than hatred between our people. And because you are here, I know this must be so." Cuchua lowered himself to the ground, cross-legged, "Now sit, and we talk more of these things."

Ethan hesitated. "I can't figure this,

Cuchua. You must've changed one hell of a lot. I heard that you rode the trail with Victorio." Even as he spoke he wondered if he was stretching his luck too far. But it didn't snap.

"I was young, then," said the Apache. "Victorio was the brother of my father. A brave warrior . . . But the *heshke* was on him, the killing curse."

"He went crazy, you mean?"

"Apache or white man," replied Cuchua. "All can have evil spirit go in them. You know this to be true."

Merle was already sitting. She pulled at Ethan's sleeve. "He's right, Ethan. You must talk to him."

Years after, in Ethan's mind, this day would take on the unreal quality of a dream. How he'd sat with the man whose very name had set his blood boiling in fury. How they'd fetched water for Merle, and a blanket from the buggy. How men who'd planned a tormenting death for the white man and woman were now treating them like guests.

Cuchua told them his story. About how things got so bad at the San Carlos Agency that he'd cut loose with some of the younger braves. They'd angled down on the edge of the mountains, into Mexico, searching for game they might hunt. His eyes burned with the love of freedom as he spoke, but it was clear that things had been no easier over the border than in the agency confines.

"The hunting was no good. And the blue-coats of the south-country hunt us as fiercely as the yellow-leg horse-soldiers. Two of my braves died in a fight with them."

Ethan's eyes went to the tall Indian who was running a finger down the livid, newly-healed scar on his face. Just the kind of wound that a sabre slice would cause. "And so you figured on coming back?" he asked.

Cuchua made a curving motion with his hand, as if to signify the route of their return. "We heard it said that a village had been attacked. We heard that Cuchua and his braves had been seen, when we knew it could not be so. And so we came to see this place."

They had read the signs as clearly as a white man could read a story in a book. The horses had been shod; Mexican style. The attackers had been armed with Winchesters. No Apache had been near this place.

"There was anger in our hearts," Cuchua continued. "And it was that anger which almost cost you and your fine woman your lives. If I had been here, this would not have been so. But I rode to speak with Chilli Woman, and my braves waited for my return."

"It's just a good job that you came back when you did," commented Ethan wryly. "So what did Chilli Woman have to say about all this? Does she figure that Garcia paid these Mexicans to finish the village?"

But it was Merle who answered. "Garcia may have hired them, but I don't believe he was in charge, Ethan." Her grey eyes stared into his. "There'd be only one reason to carry out such a wicked plan. Indian raids in this area might force the army to set up a garrison fort . . . "

He caught at her arm. "Which'd be just what Duke Oakman wanted! Hell, you're right, Merle."

He realised that Cuchua was watching them both carefully. "That is what Chilli Woman say to me. That this is work of white man called Oakman."

Turning, Ethan looked towards the graves, still not knowing which one was Sarita's resting place. It made no sense that she'd died, but in a weird way it might have been more acceptable if she had been killed in an Apache attack. After all, Indians were a kind of natural hazard of frontier life, along with cactus and rattlesnakes and all the rest.

But to be slaughtered as part of some wicked plot, all in the name of profit . . . His rage suddenly blazed hotter than the flames which must have consumed the village.

"We'll get that bastard Oakman

for this!" Impulsively he extended his hand.

Cuchua flinched back, like a man being attacked and then gave a nod of understanding. His hand closed on Ethan's. "Now we shall ride back to the agency."

"Now just a second," said Ethan. "Maybe it's all crystal clear to me. But nothing's been proved. And until it has you fellers'd best steer clear of San Carlos. 'Cause as things stand soon as you step foot there you'll be flung in the agency hoosegow. Maybe even get hung for it!"

But Cuchua stood up, and his braves followed suit. "By time we ride back into San Carlos, the truth will be known. I feel this . . . " He tapped his chest. "Here in my heart."

Ethan's protests fell on unhearing ears, and just ten minutes later and he and Merle were alone. The Indians had sifted away from them, melting into the rocky landscape to the west. Right now he couldn't think where to start. Cuchua had convinced him; but proving it to others was going to be a different sack of grain.

The plotters who'd set this up had done their work well. Tobe Wellbeloved would take a hell of a lot of convincing that he hadn't seen a bunch of Apaches; and those dying words of old Manuelo had a terrible ring of truth to them. Oakman and Garcia had Chesterville sewn up tight, and he'd already seen how tough it would be to find anybody to stand alongside him in bringing them down.

He looked at Merle. "We'd best get back to town."

She nodded wanly, and they started back for the buckboard. They'd only gone a few steps, though, when she turned on him, pressing her body against his, and hugging him so tight he could barely breathe.

"I was so frightened. I hadn't thought a person could be so scared." She placed her hands either side of his face, dragging him closer. "It was so brave what you did. Trying to stop that Indian from . . . "

Her touch had sent his skin tingling. She looked so goddamn pretty and a powerful hunger gnawed in him. He'd heard tell that escaping from some life-threatening danger could do this to a man and a woman. It was as if none of the normal rules mattered any more; that being alive, and proving it, was the most important thing.

And that same fire was kindling itself in her. Her ardent mouth was on his, and her body was moving against him. Ethan felt himself succumbing, letting desire take over from reason. And then, over Merle's shoulder he saw that neat line of mounded graves, and the spell shattered like a mirror being hit by a bullet.

He twisted away from the girl, breathless. "We gotta stop this, Merle."

Suddenly shamed, she backed away, avoiding his gaze. "I'm sorry. I don't know what came over me."

Gently he took her hand. "Came over

us both. Nobody's to blame. Another time, another place, and maybe . . . "

She pushed her hands through her tangled tresses. "I should have thought," she said shakily. "Here, in the village, you and Sarita . . . "

"Nothing to do with that," Ethan replied softly. "She's a memory now, Merle. A pretty powerful, loving memory. But she's gone." He glanced back at the graves, and his face became hard. "But there's one more thing I got to do for her, and her neighbours."

"Revenge?"

He shook his head. "Justice," he said.

★ ★ ★

Micky Gomez was sitting there with old Pauletta when they came in. He was quick to spot that they'd both just been through some ordeal. Grabbing his crutch, he heaved himself out of his chair. "What has happened, *amigo*?"

"You wouldn't believe it, Micky,"

said Ethan wearily. "We just been chinwagging with Cuchua."

Micky stared speechless, looking from one to the other, and Ethan took himself across to where the old woman sat. She was thinner than he remembered; even more wrinkled, if that was possible. A ragged, pathetic bundle of possessions sat by her chair. Yet her eyes were bright and intelligent.

She gave a little nod, and forced out a few words in English. "School ... teacher ... good to see, Ethan." She held out her pitifully thin hand, and he squeezed it.

"Good to see you, too, Pauletta."

Merle came over, and spoke softly in Spanish to the old woman, welcoming her. Pauletta studied her carefully, just as she'd scanned Ethan's face the first time Sarita had taken him to her, to get her approval. Then, like that time, her old face creased in a smile, and she nodded, and he knew that Merle had passed the test.

Micky was at his shoulder, agitated. "Tell me, Ethan, what are you talking about? How is it you have seen Cuchua and returned alive?"

"I need some coffee, Micky. Come in the kitchen and I'll tell you. We got a lot of thinking to do."

By the time he'd finished spilling out the morning's events to Micky, fortified by several cups of bitterly strong coffee, the young Mexican was fiercely convinced of Oakman's guilt. "And a man who could do this could surely murder *señor* Dale. Did you speak to *señor* Wellbeloved of these things?"

Ethan shook his head. There'd been no sign of Tobe when they'd stopped off at the mission buildings. It seemed that he'd been gone a worryingly long time, but then it came to them that only a couple of hours had passed since they'd last been here, for all that it seemed like two lifetimes strung together.

But he'd finally got round to telling

Merle about Sarita's suspicions that Chester Dale had been murdered. And she was of the same mind as Micky. It was getting easy to consider Oakman capable of any kind of twisted plot which would benefit his own ends.

"We must start a holy war," Micky declared. "Raise an army and march on Oakman's *hacienda*!"

"Oh sure," said Ethan sceptically. "And you tell me where this army comes from?"

"Once it is known what he has done . . . "

"Could make folk even warier of tangling with him," Ethan cut in. "And we've got no proof of any of this."

Micky's eyes narrowed in thought. "If we get Oakman alone, maybe we force the truth from his evil mouth."

"Threaten to skin him alive, you mean?" A shiver went through him. "Anyhow he's always got a bunch of uglies with him. Same goes for Garcia, I guess."

"Maybe there is way of getting to

Garcia when he does not have men around him," said Micky suddenly. "I have told you, of Maria, my cousin."

"Sure, you told me."

"She visits him in his rooms above the *cantina*. There is a secret back entrance." He made as if to spit, then thought better of it. "How she can sell her body to him I do not know."

"All kinds of ways to survive. Maybe it's no worse than begging for pennies." He raised a hand before the other could protest. "How often does she go to see him?"

"Most nights, before the night is old," replied Micky. "He like to be down in the *cantina* when it is busy. To keep his eyes on what is happening. He say that Maria she give him strength for the night . . . " He looked away from Ethan, ashamed for his cousin.

Ethan was thinking hard. If they could use this back way in, and Maria could keep Garcia occupied, they might be able to jump him and get him out of there before he could raise any alarm.

"You think Maria might help us?"

"*Si*, maybe . . . "

They both turned sharply, alerted by noise out in the lobby. Ethan's taut nerves twanged as Merle shrieked his name, and he hurled himself out of the kitchen.

Cory Boon was stumbling through the door; he looked a sorry sight, caked in mud, and maybe things worse than mud. He had no shirt on, and was shoeless. As they came towards him he stood there shakily, blood trickling from his nose, mingling with the filth on his face.

He said one word before he started to topple. "Oakman!"

Ethan caught him as he fell, and then a wave of revulsion went through him as he saw the raw, whiplash weals on the Easterner's back.

9

ETHAN looked in through the door of Cory's room. The wounded man was lying on his face, and Merle was just finishing dealing with his dressings. "How's he doing?"

"He's doing fine."

Her affectionate tone sent a stab of jealousy through Ethan. He couldn't shake off the memory of the two of them clinging together at the village. But he managed to give Cory a friendly grin. "Having such a good-looking nurse kinda makes up for all the pain, I daresay."

"No it doesn't," Cory responded sourly. "Did you get to tell the sheriff what those brutes did to me?"

"Well, sure, I went to tell Cutler." Ethan shrugged. "He says if you were trespassing on Oakman's land then you had to expect a little roughing up."

He flinched at the vehement oath which exploded from Cory's lips. "I wasn't trespassing. That wife of his invited me in. Mind you, I got the feeling that she was two-thirds drunk. The way she kept giggling."

"Seems she found the key to the cupboard where the bottles are kept, then," commented Ethan acidly.

"Then Oakman arrived," Cory continued. "And then I put my proposition to him, and . . . "

Merle intervened, "Now don't start going over it all again, Cory. You've got to try and forget what happened."

It was a damn fool plan Cory had hatched. Asking Oakman to nail a thousand dollars onto his price. For one thing, the girl was so fired up against Oakman she wouldn't take a million dollars from him. For another, Oakman saw his chance to send another warning their way. So Cory had got himself a beating, and a whipping, and generally been kicked around by Curly

Hicks and his cronies.

"I'll find some way of getting even with that brute," hissed Cory.

"Don't talk foolish!" Merle stood up. "You just lie there and let that sleeping draught do its work."

"I guess you're right," said Cory. "Only hope it does work, because I didn't get a wink of sleep last night."

Merle followed Ethan down the stairs. "He'll be scarred for life, you know," she murmured. "On his back."

"Sure, I know," said Ethan. "But . . . "

She glared, "Maybe he has only got himself to blame, but he meant well. And Oakman will pay for it, won't he?"

"If Oakman was fined a dollar for every piece of misery he's caused," announced Ethan harshly, "then he'd still be paying in a thousand years. 'Cept it won't be his pocket book that's troubled, just his wicked neck."

Old Pauletta was methodically sewing away at Ethan's shirt that had been ripped yesterday. Her fingers were old, but she could still handle a darning needle, and she'd insisted on earning her keep.

"I'll light the lamp," said Merle. "It's nearly evening. She won't be able to see what she's doing."

The old woman looked up as Merle came across. She smiled, and the two women exchanged a few words in Spanish. Then Merle joined Ethan by the door where he was staring out at the street. The light was starting to fade out there. "You're waiting for Micky?"

He nodded. "Just hope he can persuade that cousin of his to help us with Garcia."

"Don't build your hopes too much. She'll be terrified of something going wrong. What'd happen to her then?" She paused nervously. "And suppose you do manage to catch Garcia unawares. What makes you think you can get some kind of confession out of him?"

He slapped his hand against the butt of his sidearm. "I got this. Garcia might figure living's got the edge over dying." She looked unconvinced, and he burst out, "Hell, maybe I'll drag him away into some quiet place and . . . "

"Torture him?" she asked softly. "Like the Apaches were planning on torturing you?"

Inwardly Ethan let out an angry curse at women who had too much sweet reason in their heads. Aloud, he said, "Sometimes the threat of torture's enough."

"Only if he believes you're capable of carrying out that threat," she replied. "And just how are you and Micky going to drag Garcia into some quiet place?"

He saw a chink in her blasted logic. "Won't be just me'n Micky. Not if Tobe Wellbeloved comes along." Hopefully, he scanned the noisy street again.

"That might make it easier, I guess," Merle murmured doubtfully. And then she gave an irritated toss of her head. "And that reminds me. I should go and fetch that spyglass."

"Tobe's spyglass?" he asked in surprise. "Why'd you bring that back here?"

"I forgot to leave it when we stopped off at his place. I did have other things on my mind. Anyway, it seemed a shame not to try getting the broken lens replaced."

"Didn't reckon there was anyone in Chesterville made a living from fixing spyglasses," he remarked.

"Micky told me that the gunsmith down the street does a side trade in mending clocks and watches."

"Zeke Miller?" Ethan nodded. "Sure, I recall Chester taking his old watch down to him once or twice."

"I don't know if he can do anything," she said. "Mr Miller was out when I called. I left it with his assistant."

"How come you're so anxious to get it fixed?" Then, glad to have something to grin about, he recalled her talking about using a similar telescope when she was a child. "You doing this for Tobe, or yourself? The Lord only knows what you'd see peeking through some of the windows round here. Could be a real education."

"I've no intention of peeking, as you put it," she retorted haughtily. "If a thing's broken it needs mending. And what's so wrong in doing a favour for someone?"

"Nothing. And I'm sure Tobe'll be mighty grateful if you do get it fixed." He put a warning hand on her arm. "But there's no sense in going now, Merle. Wait till morning."

With injured dignity, she said, "If I can survive the attentions of a dozen Apaches, Ethan Winter, I can sure cope with a few drunken cowboys."

You had to admire the way her spirits kept up. "Guess you can. But you mind old Zeke Miller doesn't keep you talking too long with his yarns about old Chester. His tongue never knows when to rein itself in."

"I'll be as quick as I can." She nodded to old Pauletta, then set off down Main Street. Ethan kept his eye on her until she disappeared safely into the gunsmith's store a door or two down from the bank. He was just turning back, when he spotted Tobe heading his way, cantankerously pushing past anyone blocking his path.

"Found your message," he rumbled, as he followed Ethan inside. "Only got back to my place this afternoon."

"Where in hell you been?"

"Walking, doing a bit of shooting. Thinking."

Ethan grinned faintly, "Sounds the kind of life a feller could get used to."

"It's peaceful," grunted Tobe. "Your note didn't say much. But that's the way with your messages, ain't it?"

Ethan shrugged off that pointed reference to the note he'd left for Chester, two years before. "Thought it best not to write too much down. Set yourself down Tobe and I'll tell you all about it."

Tobe removed his beaver hat, setting it by his chair, and teased out his few remaining shreds of tobacco into a spindly smoke. He looked towards Pauletta in her corner. "What she doing here?"

Ethan explained. Tobe lit his smoke. "Got her earning her keep, then. That your shirt she's mending?"

"Got torn by one of Cuchua's braves. Down in Sarita's village yesterday."

Tobe drew on his cigarette too hard, and coughed on a lungful of smoke. "You tangled with a bunch of Apaches? Then how come you still got your hair?"

Ethan quickly got into the meat of the tale, with Tobe listening mostly without comment, just giving the odd grunt. "So what you saw wasn't Apaches. Just a half-breed and a bunch of murderous Mexes. Maybe the same ones I tangled with the other day. They must've fixed things up pretty good at the village to fool you, Tobe."

Darkly, Tobe said, "I wasn't looking

203

too close. There was dead folks to be buried. Didn't spend too much time counting empty shell-cases. Looked like Apache work to me. You reckon this Injun was telling true?"

"I reckon so."

"Well," said Tobe, "seems likely that Oakman was behind it, with him itching for the army to set up here."

"But maybe there was another reason," butted in Ethan. "Tobe, did you ever have any suspicion that Chester's death might not have been natural?"

"Death's the most unnatural thing to happen to anyone," growled Tobe. "Stops you doing natural things. Like walking and breathing."

"S'pose he'd been murdered? The doc was certain sure that he'd had a heart attack?"

"Seemed so," returned Tobe. "Mind you, doc likes his whisky. Guess he's been known to get it wrong once in a while. Like that time with Ma Petrie." He guffawed "Goes to him with an aching gut, and he tells her she's expecting another Petrie. Already had twelve. You recollect?"

"Sure," said Ethan tetchily. It was an old story; he'd heard Chester tell it more than once.

"Her near on sixty." recalled Tobe. "With her man dead three years. And here was doc suggesting she'd been . . . " he broke off. "Well, you know what I mean."

"So he could've got it wrong in Chester's case too?"

"Guess he might," conceded Tobe, his amusement faded. "I wouldn't put nothing past Oakman. Even wiping out a whole village for his own purpose." He leaned back, considering for a moment. "But with Mexes being tied up in this . . . "

Ethan cut in, "We figure that Garcia must be caught up in all this, too."

"It'd make sense, I guess. Garcia'd have the pick of all the badmen in Mex-town. The wicked helping the wicked." He was interrupted by a gabble of Spanish from the old woman.

She'd dropped her sewing and was staring at them.

"What was she saying?" queried Ethan. All he'd been able to make out was several repetitions of Garcia's name.

Tobe eyed the old woman thoughtfully. "Far as I can tell she's saying Garcia's made a pact with Satan."

Pauletta started off all over again, and Tobe frowned with concentration as he tried to understand her. He shook his head, looking back at Ethan. "That is one confused old hen. She reckons he's the feller that ran the trading post that was here before the town."

"You sure that's what she said?"

Tobe grunted dismissively. "That feller'd be over seventy now. Chester bought the trading post off of him and his missus. Pulled it down, then built this place."

"You remember him, Tobe?"

The old man grunted testily. "It's a whisky-hazy kind of recollection, but I saw a lot of him in the days before

Chester arrived here. I was drunk most of the time."

"And does Garcia look anything like that man?"

Tobe shrugged. "How in the name of the Almighty would I know? One Mex looks pretty much the same as another 'less you know them personal."

He grinned at Pauletta and said something encouraging. She gave a scornful glare, and crossed herself. "*El malo hombre*," she said. "*El diablo*, the devil." But she took up her sewing again.

"Anyhow, you got some plan for dealing with this?"

"We're going after Garcia," answered Ethan.

"Hoping he'll sing with a muzzle in his face?" Tobe frowned. "And just how you going to get past those barn-chested fellers he walks round with?"

"We know he's got himself a secret entrance to his private rooms over the *cantina*. Gets one special visitor coming in that way." He told Tobe about Maria.

"Well, a feller with his britches down is always at a kind of disadvantage."

"But it all depends on whether Maria'll help," said Ethan. "I'm just waiting on Micky getting back from seeing her. But I'd be mighty relieved to have you along on this, Tobe. Micky's got spirit . . . "

"But two legs is always better than one." Tobe reached down for his hat, and heaved himself to his feet. "I'll come along, Ethan."

"We're not going yet."

Tobe glowered. "The devil you ain't! Not till I get back. I'm just going to fetch me some more tobacco. Man'll need a good few smokes to help him through this."

Almost half an hour went by, and Ethan paced around getting fretful. Merle still hadn't come out of the gunsmith's, the moon was full up, and the noise from the street was reaching its usual level of whooping and shouting with the odd gun-shot mixed in for good measure.

Then at last Micky Gomez came swinging back in. There was an intense expression on his face. "Maria she will do it," he said swiftly. "But we must go now."

"Right now?"

The young Mexican nodded. "While I am with Maria, Garcia send a message that he want her to come to him. This is his way. He call and she must come."

"This messenger didn't see you?"

Micky shook his head impatiently, "You think I am foolish? No, he did not see me."

"And she's agreed to help?" asked Ethan.

"She know that this is the only way she have of escaping. But she will be going very soon to him."

"Better we wait for Tobe to get back," said Ethan uneasily. "Could be tricky with just the two of us."

"There is no time, *amigo*. Maria must go when he calls her. And if she is late then he . . . he hurt her."

"I guess we go now then." Pauletta watched impassively as he scribbled a hurried note for Merle and Tobe. "You'd best tell the old woman something, Micky. Nothing to worry her, though, you hear."

Micky addressed a few words to the old woman, and whatever he'd said satisfied her. Then they headed out into the noisy street. As they moved into the back alleys of the *barrio*, though, the noise diminished. There were folk about, sure, but nowhere near the crush of humanity that Ethan had encountered on his last visit here.

"Seems kinda quiet here tonight," Ethan commented, a touch uneasily. Where in hell is everyone?"

"It is still early," replied Micky. "Just keep calm, Ethan. If you look nervous when we see Maria then maybe she change her mind."

"Sure, you're right." But his anxiety returned as they passed Lizzie's eating house, which had its door closed. "Now why'd she be closed up?"

"How do I know this?" snapped Micky. "Come, down here." He led Ethan down the dark, stinking alley alongside Lizzie's place. There were shapes moving in a yard behind a ramshackle gate to the left of them.

"What the hell is that?" Ethan hissed jumpily.

"Burros. Penned in for the night-time. Can you not smell them, *amigo*?"

"This whole warren stinks!" One of the donkeys shuffling in the cramped confines of the yard let out a snorting bray of irritation at something, setting up an unholy chorus from the other animals cooped there. "Damn stupid beasts," cursed Ethan.

"They do not kill each other, like men do," retorted Micky. "Come, they will be quiet when we have gone."

And as they moved away from the gate, out into a wider alley, the burros calmed down. That unnerving silence fell again; with the clamour of the brightly lit, crowded main street strangely distant.

Ethan tensed as a shadow moved away from a nearby wall. A girl's voice spoke low. "Miguel?"

In the slanting, shifting moonlight, he saw Micky's cousin Maria. She was wearing a shabby grey dress, with a faded shawl pulled round her shoulders. Like Micky had said, she was young, and pretty. But the fleeting glance she gave Ethan showed him that her eyes were too old. Being a survivor in this part of town was a cruel business.

She murmured quickly to Micky, who turned to Ethan. "She will go up first. We wait a few minutes and she will have made sure that it is hard for Garcia to escape."

"But how's she going to do that?"

Maria turned to look at him; and there was a kind of reproach in her dark eyes. For a terrible moment he thought that somehow Sarita's ghost had taken her over. Though it was clear she had understood his question, she answered it in Spanish, spitting the words out rapidly. Then she turned and stalked off round a corner.

"What did she say?"

Micky gave a sorrowing shake of his head. "If you do not understand, *amigo*, then it is better you do not know. Let us pray that she no more needs to do such things after tonight. Come, we must go after her."

She stood waiting by a flight of stone steps as they came up to her. She held up both hands, stretching the fingers. "Ten minutes," she hissed, and for an instant there was a look of revulsion and desperation in her face. She went up the steep steps, two at a time, and they sank into the shadows, as she tapped on the door at the top. When they next looked, she had gone inside.

Neither of them spoke, pressed there against the wall. Ethan found himself willing the minutes to pass quicker, trying to not think of what Maria might be doing up there. This was going to be tough without Tobe's massive presence.

Maybe Garcia would be alone, but his people wouldn't be far away. If anything went wrong, then they'd all be in a thick stew of trouble.

Micky touched his arm urgently. "Ten minutes have gone by now, I think."

Ethan took one last look down the alley, hoping against hope to see Tobe lumbering into view. But there was nothing moving in the shadows. He took a breath, and then led the way up the narrow, unrailed steps.

He paused just a moment at the top, listening, but there was no sound from inside. It was now or never. With one hand he drew his gun, with the other he grabbed at the door handle, and threw it open, hurling himself in.

He hadn't banked on it being so brightly lit in here, and for a moment he was almost blinded, coming out of the dark. But even as his vision cleared, he knew something was horribly amiss, as he saw the guns aimed straight at him.

And there, in front of a large bed, smiling smugly between his gigantic bodyguards was Juan Garcia himself, as dapper dressed as ever. "You would be wise to drop your gun, *señor*," he said, smooth as a schoolboy's chin. "And kick it away from you. You will not escape this time."

"This time?" Ethan let the Colt fall to the thickly carpeted floor, and shoved it forward with his boot-toe.

"You killed two of my men at the village." Garcia spread his hands. "They were less than nothing. But you must pay for them with your life."

"You set up that ambush . . . ?"

He was interrupted as Micky, heedless of the pointed guns, thrust past him, with an agonised yell. "What have you done to Maria?"

Ethan became aware of a low whimpering, moaning, animal sound from over in the shadowy corner. The girl was huddled there, her face turned to the wall.

Micky didn't get far, as one of the

big Mexicans stepped into his path, yanking the crutch away from him. For a moment, Micky balanced, desperately trying to get a hand over to the wall to steady himself, and then the man kicked viciously at his leg, sending him sprawling heavily.

"You must help my cousin," Micky blurted out from where he lay. "What have you done to her?"

Garcia looked across at him arrogantly. "Nobody tries to make a fool of Juan Garcia without paying the price." He strode away from his bodyguards, and grabbed at the girl's dress. "The whore will make few *dineros* now, with a face like this!"

He heaved Maria to her feet, forcing her round. Ethan winced at the bloody mask which the girl's face had become. "You bastards!" he spat. "Why'd you do that to her?"

Garcia laughed. "The pretty *señorita* she was so nervous. I knew she had something on her mind. She soon tell us we are to have visitors."

"You lie!" Maria's eyes were fiery with a mixture of loathing and pain, and then the shoulder of her dress ripped as she sharply pulled herself away, staggering forward towards where Ethan stood.

Garcia laughed again, "The *Americano* cannot help you, whore!"

His bodyguards joined in the mocking laughter, and were distracted just long enough to allow Maria to fall to her knees and grab for Ethan's discarded gun, and twist round with it, pointing it straight at her torturer.

It was like a long, frozen moment, and then it shattered as two bellowing shots sounded so close on each other that they might have been one. The heavy calibre slug which blazed from the Mexican's gun sent Maria flailing back against Ethan.

But her own shot had hit its target. Garcia pressed both hands to his chest as a surge of crimson welled through. He reeled back and sat on the edge of the bed staring down in stupefaction.

You could have sliced the dazed silence with a knife as the sour smell of gunsmoke mingled with the sweeter, sickly smell of blood. Micky was scrambling towards his cousin, yelling incoherently as Ethan crouched down by her, looking into that bruised and broken face. "I told them nothing . . ." was her dying whisper.

Out of the corner of his eye Ethan saw one of the huge Mexicans aiming at him. He snatched for the pistol which had fallen from Maria's hand, and triggered twice, sending the heavy man into a spin which ended in him crashing into the far door of the room.

Almost in the same moment the second of the bodyguards went toppling as Micky, ignored for a moment, got his crutch hooked round the man's ankle. Then with a roar of vengeful rage he scrambled on top of him, and pulled a knife from his belt. It flashed once, twice, and the hulk's throat was slashed from ear to ear, giving him a scarlet scarf which grew wider by the moment.

Footsteps were pounding up the inner staircase now. Garcia was hunched forward on the edge of the bed, the floor round his feet slippery with his own blood. Ethan yanked up the slumped head, and looked into eyes which were starting to glaze with approaching death. His heart sank; making threats to a dying man would be no more effective than spitting into a hurricane.

Those outside were hammering violently on the door now, trying to get it open, but the weight of the dead man lying it was wedging it as tight as if it was locked.

"You're dying, Garcia," he hissed. "Why not make your confession to me?"

Garcia gave a bloodily-flecked cough. "Confess to you? You are no *padre*."

"I'm the best you're going to get! You were in on the murder of Chester, weren't you?"

A series of heavy blows on the blocked door told Ethan that someone was taking a hammer to it, and it was beginning to splinter under the wild battering. They were running out of time. And he couldn't believe that nobody else knew about the back entrance into Garcia's rooms.

"Micky!" he yelled, "get hold of a gun and send a few shots into the door!" Garcia was swaying now, and would have fallen but for Ethan holding him up. "You and Oakman set up Chester's murder, didn't you? And that phoney Indian raid on the village?"

Micky blasted off a rattle of gunshots at the door, and for a moment the agitated crowd outside fell back. "We must get out, Ethan!" he shouted.

"You get yourself out, Micky!"

"I shall not leave you!"

"Just git!" Without turning to see whether the young man obeyed his order, he moved his face close to Garcia's. The man could die any moment. "You and Oakman? That's all I want to know, Garcia."

There was a terrible glassiness in the

man's stare, and for a moment Ethan believed he must have died already. And then Garcia nodded. "*Si*. Duke Oakman and Garcia . . . "

The attack on the door had begun again with renewed vigour. Garcia muttered a few words in Spanish; something about his mother, and the death shudder went through him. Ethan let go of him, and he fell back onto the bed, eyes staring sightlessly at the ceiling.

At the same moment the inner door gave way. Ethan emptied his revolver towards it, and threw himself towards the open door. Thankfully, there was no sign of Micky.

But as he reached the top of the steps, his way was blocked by two men coming the other way. The force of his approach caught them unawares and he shouldered into the first, sending him sideways off the edge. The other man was still there though, his gun poised, and the room behind him was a sea of noise.

He had no choice but to jump. He hurled himself off, and landed square on the man he'd pushed off, ending his attempts to get back to his feet. Winded by the fall, Ethan began to run. The man on the steps fired, and the shots whined past his ears. His pursuers were all coming down the steps now, and he knew that there'd be at least half a dozen guns trained on his back. He'd got what he wanted out of Garcia, but it seemed that he was never going to be able to tell anyone.

10

"**G**ET against the wall, Ethan!" Micky's yell had come from the corner of the alley. Ethan flattened back just as a whirl of panicked burros stampeded by; a dozen or more, braying wildly, hooves flailing, rushing straight into the mob pursuing him.

He didn't look back to see the havoc that the frightened animals were causing in the narrow alley, though he could hear the screeching alarm well enough. He just headed on, almost colliding with Micky, who grabbed at his arm. "This way, Ethan!"

For a man with one leg, he put on quite a turn of speed, and they were soon almost into the safety of Main Street. 'Course, there could be plenty of trouble looming. Oakman would be less than happy to have lost his

Mexican sidekick; but that worry was for later.

Breathless, Ethan slowed. "How'd you get those burros to stampede, Micky?"

Micky turned, gazing back. "I threw a match into their straw. All animals they fear fire." He looked at Ethan. "Did Garcia tell you anything?"

"Sure. Him and Oakman, like we thought." He shrugged. "I mean, we got nothing in writing. But knowing the truth's half-way to proving it, I guess."

They walked on, slower. Nobody on the bustling street gave them a second glance. The din out here would have been enough to drown the sound of gunfire from back in the *barrio*. Ethan had seen plenty of evidence about how little the Main Street inhabitants worried about their poorer neighbours, so they wouldn't be overly disturbed by a few Mexicans shooting each other.

"They beat Maria wickedly," muttered Micky. "She would not have betrayed us otherwise."

"She didn't betray us," said Ethan sharply. "She was a brave girl. And she took Garcia with her."

Micky nodded. "I am sorry I had to leave her there."

"You had no choice, *amigo*. As to how they knew we were coming, Garcia has . . . had, eyes and ears everywhere."

They paused on the hotel steps. "But what happens now? Garcia is dead, but there is still Oakman. And there will be others willing to work for him in the *barrio* . . . "

"Sure. So we got to figure out how to finish Oakman." As he came through the door, some sixth sense told Ethan something was wrong; there was a chill, prickly atmosphere in there. He began moving to where Merle and old Pauletta were sitting on the far side. "Something happened while I've been gone?" he demanded.

Merle started to speak, "Ethan, it's . . . "

"Glad to see you fellers got back

in one piece." Tobe Wellbeloved had stepped out of the shadows, and now he slammed the door shut, pressing his back to it. "Guess that means that you dealt with Garcia, then?"

Ethan twisted round uncertainly. "He's dead, Tobe. And where in hell did you get to . . . ?" His voice tailed off as he saw the gun in the old man's hand. "What's going on, Tobe. Why you hefting that?"

Now Merle leapt to her feet, pointing at Tobe. "He's been working for Garcia! You thought he was your friend but he was . . . "

Scowling, Tobe raised his heavy .44, pointing it unwaveringly at the two men. "Jus' you and Micky set down nice and easy."

His heart thudding like a steam-hammer, Ethan edged back and found himself a chair. "Tobe, she can't be right. Merle's got it all wrong. Tell me!"

"She's wrong 'bout one thing," snapped Tobe. "Juan Garcia was working for me! And now you gone and killed him." His eyes flickered over Merle. "Just a pity that you ever picked up that spyglass."

"What in hell's the spyglass got to do with anything?" Ethan almost shouted.

Merle looked round fearfully. "The gunsmith said Tobe asked him to put in a new lens just after Christmas. He couldn't get hold of one. The 'scope has been useless since then. I didn't think anything of it until I gave it back."

"What're you talking about?" Ethan blurted out.

"If it's been broken since Christmas then he couldn't have seen Apaches through it just a couple of months ago."

Tobe chuckled. "Could see in her eyes that she knowed. So I reckoned that her time in Chesterville was just about done." He shook his head. "Course, I figured that you and Micky wouldn't be coming back. I give Garcia plenty of warning that you was coming."

"Garcia told me he was working for Oakman," Ethan burst out "With his dying breath!"

"Like I always say," said Tobe. "Never trust a Mex! Hell, when it comes to it, never trust nobody." He leaned against the door. "Guess I'll have to manage without Garcia now. And without you folks, too."

Then he laughed, a crazy kind of laugh, and Ethan's blood ran cold. "I still can't believe that you were behind the massacre, Tobe."

"Just stay calm, Ethan boy." Tobe sniffed. Sure, they all died. But quick. And there weren't no torturing. They died clean, and we buried them quick, like I planned."

Bile rose in Ethan's throat. "In the name of the Almighty, why'd you do it?"

Tobe looked almost sorrowful. "Thing was, Sarita she came to my place after she seen that feller riding through the village. Wanted to ask my advice, I guess. Real shame that she caught me chinwagging with that same feller and with Garcia. Brighter than a bole full of glow-worms was Sarita. Not hard for her to figure out that I'd had something to do with Chester's death myself."

Micky let out a bellow of anguished fury, and shoved himself to his feet, pouring out a string of curses in Tobe's direction. Old Pauletta said something sharp to him, and dragged him back into his seat.

"Course," returned Tobe. "Didn't reckon the truth'd stay hid for ever. And once folk figured it wasn't Injuns done it, then the finger'd soon get pointed at Oakman."

Everyone always said if a madman was set on killing you, then you kept him talking. "How'd you make Chester's death look like a heart-attack, Tobe?" asked Ethan.

"Didn't need to. The Mex climbed into his room after he'd been drinking heavy, and smothered him with his pillow. I got doc so drunk he'd have said it was heart-failure even if Chester had a dozen slugs in him!"

His craggy face was hard as granite. "We're all reaping a harvest of evil. Chesterville was born on a lie, built on murder, and now it's skittering on the edge of the chasm of Hell. Just wish Chester was here to see it."

Ethan snatched at one phrase, "Built on murder?"

Tobe gave a mocking chuckle. "Everyone reckons Chester bought the trading post off the feller that ran it. Real anxious to buy, but the feller kept upping his price."

Pausing, he scanned his audience with glittering eyes. "So Chester killed him. Would've killed his missus too, I daresay, only somehow she managed to escape. He's buried under this place, deep down. And you folks'll soon be joining him there."

Something here didn't quite make sense to Ethan. Maybe Tobe had just snapped, or maybe there was some logic in all the things he'd done. "Seems you feel pretty sore about Chester, then, Tobe?"

Tobe eyed him sharply. "And I got reason. Chester said it was *me* killed the feller in a drink-sodden rage."

"And you believed him?"

"Hell, those days are just a whisky blur to me. A man does murder, he should be punished. My punishment was to stay here, helping Chester build up this damnation town!"

To Ethan, there seemed to be more noise than usual drifting in from Main Street; a lot of shouting and screeching going on about something. If Tobe blasted off at them now, nobody was going to hear, or care, if they did. Keeping him distracted was the surest way of staying alive just a little longer.

"So when did you find out that you'd been blackmailed for something you'd never done?"

"When Juan Garcia arrived in town. Must've been fate brung him to my place first, asking if Chester Dale was still alive." Tobe looked towards Pauletta and gave a grim smile. "That old gal ain't so stupid. She'd never seen him before, but he looked the spit of his pa. So you think how I felt, seeing a dead man standing at my door!"

"Garcia's father was the trading post owner?" Ethan burst out. "Is that what you're saying?"

"Just that," Tobe confirmed. "The woman who ran off, back to Mexico, she was six months gone. She done well by her son, brought him up proper, good schooling and all." For a moment he looked regretful. "Could tell that from how he talked. But she fed a fearsome hate in him about the man killed his pa. Set a lot of store by revenge, do Mexes."

The gun's weight was telling on his ageing muscles, and he rested it down for a moment. He was listening. "What's all that ruckus out there?"

"It's nothing, Tobe," said Ethan. Out of the corner of his eye he'd seen a movement at the top of the staircase. "So Garcia told you what really happened?"

"All those years!" Tobe bellowed out. "Finding out that all those years I'd worked for Chester 'cause of a murderous lie. That's when I knew I'd bring this town down, and everyone in it. Helped Garcia set himself up in Mex-town. And he's sure made things bad for them. And got rid of Chester, so's Oakman could lead us all into perdition."

"And made sure that a lot of innocent people got tormented and murdered?" blurted out Merle. "What kind of justice is that?"

"No justice at all!"

Cory Boon had spoken from the top of the stairs. Staggering slightly, still weak from his wounds, he moved into view. Tobe was startled; he'd clearly forgotten all about Cory's presence in the hotel. It took him only a second or two to recover from the surprise, and he wheeled the gun up towards the Easterner. But the delay had been long enough to allow Ethan to hurl himself across the lobby and close with the old man.

"You're making a mistake, Ethan!" Tobe's gun hand swung round, and Ethan grunted with pain as the muzzle lashed viciously across his cheek. He tried to grab the old man's wrist, but Tobe jammed an elbow into his chest, just below his throat, and Ethan lurched back, seeing stars, as the .44 twisted back in his direction.

The door suddenly burst open. "You've got to get out of here, the whole town's catching fire!" The man in the doorway, dishevelled and agitated, was Mr Shelby the bank president. "Fire!" he shouted again.

Tobe let out a mighty roar of triumph. "Hellfire's a-coming. Glory be! The Day of Judgement's here already." He let off a couple of shots into the air, bringing plaster down round his ears, and darted off, like a man half his age, up the stairs.

Cory was midway down. He made

an ineffective grab at the old man, and Tobe threw a savage punch at him, catching him on the side of the head and sending him rolling painfully down the rest of the stairs.

Ethan gathered his wits, as Merle went to help the moaning Cory. He could smell the smog now. He stared confusedly at Mr Shelby, who was gazing nonplussed at Tobe's departing figure. "How bad's this fire?"

"Pretty bad, Mr Winter. Started in the Mexican quarter. With the wind getting up, it's spreading like the plague down this side of the street."

There was a devilishly flickering reddish glow spreading over Main Street. Already some of the buildings closest to the edge of the *barrio* were afire, and the dry wind was fanning the blaze to a fury, sending sparks showering everywhere.

Ethan helped Merle drag Cory outside. The scene out there was a maelstrom of shouting, screaming hysteria. Horses tied to saloon hitching rails reared and kicked in fear of the onrushing flames. Animals which had broken free galloped wildly amongst the panicky crowds of people.

Over at one of the saloons, a fat man dressed only in a towel leapt from a first floor window, cannoning into the stream of drunks and gamblers belatedly surging out. There seemed to be shrieking saloon girls running everywhere. Some of them were half-dressed, followed by their sheepish customers, struggling to get back into their clothes. One bunch of poker players dragged a table out into the middle of the chaotic street, before calmly settling down to finish their interrupted hand.

"We've got to stop it spreading over the other side of the street!" yelled Shelby, sidestepping a man who ran by in a frenzy, slapping at his burning britches with his hat, before diving into the nearest water trough.

"Not a lot anyone can do," Ethan shouted above the din. "Saw a fire like this once before. Town in Texas. Tinder-dry like this one. Burned to a crisp!"

Fire was a hungry, scavenging beast, gulping down one meal then moving on ravenously to consume the next. Already a canvas canopy over the front of a feed-store on the other side of the street had caught light. The desperate merchant and his family were making near-hopeless efforts to quench the flames.

Clouds of black, stinking, choking smoke were rolling over them now. A saloon only two doors down from the hotel was already beginning to burn, and now waves of scorching heat were starting to hit them.

Shelby and a couple of other businessmen were trying to rally some sort of effort to get things under control. But those who'd been in the saloons scurried by unheeding, and those escaping from the engulfing inferno of the barrio just gave looks of withering contempt.

One man stopped though; his face smoke-blackened, and one hand badly burned. "You ask my help now, *señor*?" It was the Mexican Ethan had seen in the bank. "Do they not say men reap the harvest of their deeds?" Then clutching his pathetic bundle of possessions he hurried on to the safety of the open land outside town.

"This must be what hell looks like," cried Merle, still supporting a half-sagging Cory.

"Maybe it's just like Tobe says, and this is hellfire coming to Chesterville! Like the pictures Oakman's wife saw in her cards. Come on. Let's get out of here."

"If we all pull together," Shelby screamed, "we can save half the town!"

"Is it worth saving?" Ethan fired back. He and Merle began to haul Cory along between them, and then he stared. There were lights out beyond the edge of town, where the crowd was gathering to watch Chesterville burn. A line of moving, flickering lights, as if the fire was trying to surround them from both sides.

They reached open ground, and laid Cory down. Ethan could see them coming now; men carrying flaring torches, led by a massive figure mounted on a mournful mule. Fifty or sixty Mexicans, hurrying now. And in a straggling resentful line, pushed and goaded like steers to the slaughter, he saw Duke Oakman, Curly Hicks, his arm still bandaged, and the rest of those mean-minded hired hands who'd run wild as they pleased in the town.

The mule reached him, and he looked into the dark eyes of Lizzie, Chilli Woman, as Cuchua had called her. Realization hit him. That's why the *barrio* had seemed so deserted. "You decided to go after Oakman yourself?"

With difficulty the large woman dismounted. Someone was dragging a bedraggled Oakman over to her. "We knew that *Americano* justice would be no good to us," she said.

"This man destroy a village. You know this."

Oakman's fine clothes were ripped and filthy. "I had nothing to do with those Mexes being killed out there. This is an outrage."

Another figure stumbled forward, and Ethan's eyes narrowed as he saw the unlovely face of Sheriff Cutler staring at him. "Unlucky time for you to go a-visiting your boss, Cutler."

Lizzie spat on the ground. "This is the man who has sworn to keep the law. And he laugh and drink with the biggest breaker of laws."

Cutler found his voice. "They'll all hang for this!"

"You're just lucky they didn't string you up back there," commented Ethan. He turned to the woman. "We all got one thing wrong: Oakman wasn't responsible for the massacre. But I'd say there's plenty more he did do." He waved his hand back towards the town. "And his empire's burning. He's finished, one way or the other, Lizzie."

She stared at him, confused. "You saying he didn't do that massacre, then who . . . ?"

But she was interrupted as the wretched figure of Shelby came running up. "Listen. We've got a chance to save Chesterville. If enough of us form a chain we can stop it spreading. Please!"

Lizzie glowered at the banker. "My people have lost everything they owned. Why should we wish to stop you losing all that you own, *señor presidente*?"

Shelby folded his hands like a man praying. "Things will be different after this. I give you my word," he gabbled. "The saloons have gone. Chesterville will be a decent town. We'll help you, I promise. Won't we, Mr Winter?" He turned his pleading eyes on Ethan. "Tell them!"

"Don't know why they should listen to me," said Ethan. "I'm an *Americano*, too."

Lizzie had a group of her followers clustered round her now, all trying to get her attention. She looked an unlikely sort of general; but she had a general's way of commanding. She silenced their noise with a shout. "We want justice!" she said. "We want to be treated fair. We want the evil men to be punished."

Suddenly her huge hand reached out and snatched the star still pinned to Cutler's shirt. The fabric ripped as it came away. Her gaze raked Ethan, and then she thrust the silver badge towards him. "If this is on your chest, mister, then maybe we got some hope."

He held it in his hand, weighing it, looking back at the blaze, and the running, futile figures trying to prevent it spreading. And then there was a cry from Merle which cut through the clamour. "Up there! On the hotel roof!"

Everyone stared towards the hotel which had been the first building to rise in the town. There was a figure standing astride high up, his arms spread wide. Behind him smoke and flames danced in an ecstasy of destruction. The lower and mid floors of the hotel were blazing already, and flames were licking avidly round him. Tobe Wellbeloved knew he was being watched. He waved his arms in diabolical joy, doing a crazy dance up there on the fire-hot shingles.

Everyone who'd made Chesterville what it was, what it had become, stood in silence as they gazed at him. He took off that familiar tall beaver hat and hurled it high to the glowing sky. Long after, there'd be those who swore they'd heard him laughing like a demon from the pit.

Then suddenly, further along from him, the fire broke through the roof in a spurting gush, and the timbers began to give way. Afterwards some said Tobe had been plucked from the roof by some devilish hand, soaring off into the fiery sky. But nobody ever saw him again.

Ethan knew what he had to do. He

pinned the lawman's star on his own shirt. "Let's go!" he shouted. "Tobe wanted this town destroyed. Let's make good and sure that he doesn't get his way!"

11

THE man in the expensive city suit stepped out of the Wells Fargo depot, and blinked in the strong sunlight. He still felt half-asleep; the stage had been well-sprung and had lulled him into a doze despite the unevenness of the rocky trail. He yawned, stretching, and then someone tapped him on the shoulder.

"Hey mister, forgot your change. Only a quarter for minding your trunk."

He turned, reaching out, and then another hand reached over above his and grabbed the change from the clerk. "Seems I heard that once before, sometime."

Ethan Winter grinned at the startled new arrival. "How you doing, Cory?"

Cory Boon let out a laugh, and thrust out his hand. "Hi there. Long time no see."

Ethan made to pocket the change, and then gave it to Cory. "Five years? Or is it six?"

"Nearer five, I'd say." The silver star on the other man's shirt glinted in the sun. "And you're still the lawman round here?"

"Not for much longer. I figure it's time I gave somebody else the chance."

The Fargo clerk was still standing there. "Sometimes wonder why we need a sheriff here. This town's the sleepiest I ever worked in. Especially this time o'day with everyone taking a siesta."

"Is that why the place looks so empty? You just think yourself lucky. I remember . . . " Cory stopped. "Well, the past is gone."

His eyes were getting used to the bright light now, and he was taking in the scene over the far side of the street. In one glance he took in a large general store, a building announcing itself to be the home of the *Chesterfield Herald*, and . . . He blinked. "Am I imagining it, or is that a church you've got across there?"

"Busiest place in town on a Sunday." Ethan reached down, picking up Cory's carpet bag. For a moment he recalled the weight of that bag he'd carried with him all those years ago. This was light enough.

"Still got a couple of saloons, though, I see," commented the Easterner as they made off down the street.

"Hell, I take a drink in there myself," protested Ethan. "Though even I got to leave my gun at the door."

Cory came to a halt. "Well, looks like you've put things back together. Last time I looked over there it was just a charred ruin."

"The Great Fire of Chesterville," muttered Ethan. "Well, it kind of brought the town together, you might say. Those folk who mattered, anyhow." He paused, "Now. Cory. How's that wife of yours? Thought you were fixing on bringing her along."

Cory grinned. "Oh she was all eager

to come. Then we found she was, expecting."

With a little whoop, Ethan slapped the other man on the shoulder. "You old dog! Why didn't you say before? About time, too. Still, a real shame she couldn't come with you."

"I know. But I thought if I'd put off coming back again, it might be another five years before I got here."

"Business going well?"

"Cut-throat," replied Cory. "That's real estate for you, though. Up in New York. But I always think that the lessons I learned down here taught me how to be tougher than the next man." He smiled, "Though it'd be real nice to sit out on a rocking chair in the sun and just let the world go lazily by. Maybe we'll come live here when I retire."

Ethan nodded. "Not such a bad idea. Hell, some people say it's just too damn sleepy here, but I like it that way. Not what Chester Dale intended maybe, but then I guess he got a lot of things wrong. Which was why in the end Tobe Wellbeloved was able to work so much wicked mischief."

A smart buckboard was heading down the street towards them; the horses sleek and shining despite the ever-present dust. Cory shaded his eyes. "That isn't . . . ?"

The buggy came to a halt, and the driver swung down, walking towards them with an oddly stiff gait. Micky Gomez grinned at Cory's wide-eyed astonishment. "You think I have grown new leg?"

He hitched up one leg of his smart britches a little, displaying a beautifully carved wooden leg. "Maybe not so good as a real one. But when it wear out I just get a new one made for myself!"

"Well, I'm glad to see you looking so well," said Cory. "And I hear you're doing real well in business."

"Best horse-breeder in the South-West," Micky nodded proudly. "I got twenty men working for me. All

Mexican-American. Though none can break a horse like I could." He paused, reflective just for a moment. Then he brisked himself up. "I got work to do. Everyone else take siesta, Micky Gomez has to be busy. I see you later, *señor* Boon."

He walked with that rolling gait back to his buckboard, and pulled himself agilely aboard, setting off at a fast clip. "Good to see he's done so well."

Ethan nodded. "You'll be getting the feeling that there's not a single problem in Chesterville, Cory."

"And I might be right."

"Well, folk have their worries, like everywhere else. I guess they just don't seem to matter so much out here." They walked on. "But you'll have to ride out and see the village. Wouldn't believe how it's grown. It'll be rivalling this place soon."

Cory glanced back towards the disappearing buckboard. "Micky's stopped blaming himself for causing the fire?"

Ethan shrugged. "For a while, it brought him low. But he scattered those burros to save my life. And nobody knows for certain it was him started it. A few lives were lost, sure, but not so many. And it burned out the evil. He looks at it that way, now."

He stopped. "Well I guess you'd like to book in to your hotel, Cory."

It was there, where it had always been, on the intersection of the two roads. Not that there was much traffic from the west now. No-one had worked the timber slopes since Oakman had been hauled off to the penitentiary in Prescott after a trial which detailed more crimes and illegal activities than anyone had thought possible. The slopes had been getting depleted anyhow, which was one reason Oakman had been spreading his net. There'd been plenty of takers for the Triple-O spread, when Lucinda Oakman put it up for sale, but everyone figured the risk of working the slopes wasn't worth it.

Cory stared long and hard at the hotel building. "Doesn't look that much different, from before."

"The builders followed Tobe's plans," Ethan told him. "He may have been crazy at the end, but he knew something about building."

"Don't people think it's kind of unlucky, though?" asked the man from New York. "Haunted, jinxed, whatever?"

"That'd be foolish," returned Ethan. "As foolish as thinking that some old Injun legend about this being an evil place had any credit to it. There's good growing land, sure, and terrain where even weeds won't take root. But evil lies in men, not in land."

"Guess that's right." Cory stared up at the wide board stretched between the first and second floors. "And with a change of name . . ." He broke off as he saw a figure appear at the door. She was suddenly dashing towards them, her skirts flying. A tiny figure came down the steps after; a little boy, wailing like he'd been abandoned, his chubby legs moving as quick as they could.

A moment later and Cory was being hugged tightly. "What're you standing out here for!" she exclaimed, half-laughing, half-crying, and glared at Ethan. "Has this lawman been raking up old arguments with you?"

"The sheriff doesn't argue with folk," said Ethan with a grin. "Got to be impartial in upholding the law. And your other customers are going to be mighty jealous seeing you treating this one like this, Merle."

The child had reached them now. He came up behind Merle and tugged anxiously at her skirts. "Mammy come back!" he complained bitterly.

She looked down at him. "Now what has gotten into you, Benjamin? I wasn't running off. Just saying howdy to your Uncle Cory here. You go bother someone else."

Ethan laughed, and swung the youngster up in one arm, and picked

Cory's bag up with his other hand. "Something you can't learn early enough," he said to his son, as he strode off. "When a woman tells you to do something, you jump!"

He looked up for a moment, at the elegantly painted sign above the door. "*The Hotel Sarita*," he murmured. Hadn't been his idea; that. Merle had suggested it on the day of their wedding. And it was a good name. He'd come back here, looking for Sarita. When he hadn't found her, for a while he'd reckoned his life might not be worth living. Sarita would have told him how foolish he was being to think like that. And she'd have been as right as she always was.

Other titles in the
Linford Western Library:

TOP HAND
Wade Everett

The Broken T was big. But no ranch is big enough to let a man hide from himself.

GUN WOLVES OF LOBO BASIN
Lee Floren

The Feud was a blood debt. When Smoke Talbot found the outlaws who gunned down his folks he aimed to nail their hide to the barn door.

SHOTGUN SHARKEY
Marshall Grover

The westbound coach carrying the indomitable Larry and Stretch headed for a shooting showdown.

FIGHTING RAMROD
Charles N. Heckelmann

Most men would have cut their losses, but Frazer counted the bullets in his guns and said he'd soak the range in blood before he'd give up another inch of what was his.

LONE GUN
Eric Allen

Smoke Blackbird had been away too long. The Lequires had seized the Blackbird farm, forcing the Indians and settlers off, and no one seemed willing to fight! He had to fight alone.

THE THIRD RIDER
Barry Cord

Mel Rawlins wasn't going to let anything stand in his way. His father was murdered, his two brothers gone. Now Mel rode for vengeance.

ARIZONA DRIFTERS
W. C. Tuttle

When drifting Dutton and Lonnie Steelman decide to become partners they find that they have a common enemy in the formidable Thurston brothers.

TOMBSTONE
Matt Braun

Wells Fargo paid Luke Starbuck to outgun the silver-thieving stagecoach gang at Tombstone. Before long Luke can see the only thing bearing fruit in this eldorado will be the gallows tree.

HIGH BORDER RIDERS
Lee Floren

Buckshot McKee and Tortilla Joe cut the trail of a border tough who was running Mexican beef into Texas. They stopped the smuggler in his tracks.

BRETT RANDALL, GAMBLER
E. B. Mann

Larry Day had the choice of running away from the law or of assuming a dead man's place. No matter what he decided he was bound to end up dead.

THE GUNSHARP
William R. Cox

The Eggerleys weren't very smart. They trained their sights on Will Carney and Arizona's biggest blood bath began.

THE DEPUTY OF SAN RIANO
Lawrence A. Keating and
Al. P. Nelson

When a man fell dead from his horse, Ed Grant was spotted riding away from the scene. The deputy sheriff rode out after him and came up against everything from gunfire to dynamite.

FARGO: MASSACRE RIVER
John Benteen

The ambushers up ahead had now blocked the road. Fargo's convoy was a jumble, a perfect target for the insurgents' weapons!

SUNDANCE: DEATH IN THE LAVA
John Benteen

The Modoc's captured the wagon train and its cargo of gold. But now the halfbreed they called Sundance was going after it . . .

HARSH RECKONING
Phil Ketchum

Five years of keeping himself alive in a brutal prison had made Brand tough and careless about who he gunned down . . .

FARGO: PANAMA GOLD
John Benteen

With foreign money behind him, Buckner was going to destroy the Panama Canal before it could be completed. Fargo's job was to stop Buckner.

FARGO: THE SHARPSHOOTERS
John Benteen

The Canfield clan, thirty strong were raising hell in Texas. Fargo was tough enough to hold his own against the whole clan.

PISTOL LAW
Paul Evan Lehman

Lance Jones came back to Mustang for just one thing — revenge! Revenge on the people who had him thrown in jail.

HELL RIDERS
Steve Mensing

Wade Walker's kid brother, Duane, was locked up in the Silver City jail facing a rope at dawn. Wade was a ruthless outlaw, but he was smart, and he had vowed to have his brother out of jail before morning!

DESERT OF THE DAMNED
Nelson Nye

The law was after him for the murder of a marshal — a murder he didn't commit. Breen was after him for revenge — and Breen wouldn't stop at anything . . . blackmail, a frameup . . . or murder.

DAY OF THE COMANCHEROS
Steven C. Lawrence

Their very name struck terror into men's hearts — the Comancheros, a savage army of cutthroats who swept across Texas, leaving behind a bloodstained trail of robbery and murder.

SUNDANCE: SILENT ENEMY
John Benteen

A lone crazed Cheyenne was on a personal war path. They needed to pit one man against one crazed Indian. That man was Sundance.

LASSITER
Jack Slade

Lassiter wasn't the kind of man to listen to reason. Cross him once and he'll hold a grudge for years to come — if he let you live that long.

LAST STAGE TO GOMORRAH
Barry Cord

Jeff Carter, tough ex-riverboat gambler, now had himself a horse ranch that kept him free from gunfights and card games. Until Sturvesant of Wells Fargo showed up.

McALLISTER ON THE COMANCHE CROSSING
Matt Chisholm

The Comanche, McAllister owes them a life — and the trail is soaked with the blood of the men who had tried to outrun them before.

QUICK-TRIGGER COUNTRY
Clem Colt

Turkey Red hooked up with Curly Bill Graham's outlaw crew. But wholesale murder was out of Turk's line, so when range war flared he bucked the whole border gang alone . . .

CAMPAIGNING
Jim Miller

Ambushed on the Santa Fe trail, Sean Callahan is saved by two Indian strangers. But there'll be more lead and arrows flying before the band join Kit Carson against the Comanches.

GUNSLINGER'S RANGE
Jackson Cole

Three escaped convicts are out for revenge. They won't rest until they put a bullet through the head of the dirty snake who locked them behind bars.

RUSTLER'S TRAIL
Lee Floren

Jim Carlin knew he would have to stand up and fight because he had staked his claim right in the middle of Big Ike Outland's best grass.

THE TRUTH ABOUT SNAKE RIDGE
Marshall Grover

The troubleshooters came to San Cristobal to help the needy. For Larry and Stretch the turmoil began with a brawl and then an ambush.

WOLF DOG RANGE
Lee Floren

Will Ardery would stop at nothing, unless something stopped him first — like a bullet from Pete Manly's gun.

DEVIL'S DINERO
Marshall Grover

Plagued by remorse, a rich old reprobate hired the Texas Trouble-shooters to deliver a fortune in greenbacks to each of his victims.

GUNS OF FURY
Ernest Haycox

Dane Starr, alias Dan Smith, wanted to close the door on his past and hang up his guns, but people wouldn't let him.

DONOVAN
Elmer Kelton

Donovan was supposed to be dead. Uncle Joe Vickers had fired off both barrels of a shotgun into the vicious outlaw's face as he was escaping from jail. Now Uncle Joe had been shot — in just the same way.

CODE OF THE GUN
Gordon D. Shirreffs

MacLean came riding home, with saddle tramp written all over him, but sewn in his shirt-lining was an Arizona Ranger's star.

GAMBLER'S GUN LUCK
Brett Austen

Gamblers seldom live long. Parker was a hell of a gambler. It was his life — or his death . . .